makeover

Kate Petty

Dolphin Paperbacks

First published in Great Britain in 2004
by Dolphin paperbacks
an imprint of Orion Children's Books
a division of the Orion Publishing Group Ltd
Orion House
5 Upper St Martin's Lane
London   WC2H 9EA

A catalogue record for this book is
available from the British Library

Printed in Great Britain by
Clays Ltd, St Ives plc

ISBN 1 84255 262 7

makeover

Also by Kate Petty

Summer Heat

For younger readers

The Nightspinners

Chapter One

"Well? What do you think?"

Sarah walked all round Lianne. Twice. The new top matched the grey-blue of her eyes exactly and the jeans were a perfect fit. Her fine brown hair was lifted off her face and held back with sparkly clips. The make-up was brilliant, too – very subtle. Now Lianne looked as if she had flawless skin, huge eyes, long eyelashes and full lips. The transformation was incredible. "Brilliant!"

"Isn't it amazing?" Lianne did a twirl. "The makeover people were just so cool, Sarah," she said as they went upstairs to her bedroom. "I had the best time. It's the most expensive salon in Cobford. You should have been there." She had the grace to give Sarah a rueful grin.

"Yeah, right. Like you were so quick to invite me along," Sarah said in mock anger. She'd entered Lianne for a magazine's "Best Mates Makeover" feature on the assumption that Lianne would do the same for her. Somehow Lianne had not only won the makeover, but also forgotten her part of the deal. That was typical of Lianne – so it was lucky that Sarah was easy-going. It rarely occurred to her to *mind* the high-handed way Lianne behaved. And, she had to admit, she was knocked out by the result.

Lianne Bartlett and Sarah Gray, more often known as the single item Lianne-and-Sarah, were definitely the coolest girls in their year at King Edward's. That didn't mean they were the nicest. But it meant they had the edge. Lianne was sharp and mouthy, quick off the mark. She somehow always looked right – even before the makeover. Sarah was the stunning one (though she never seemed aware of it), and Lianne needed her, needed to be part of a good-looking pair. Always a laugh, Lianne worked hard at being popular, gaining respect. Sarah simply went along with it. They'd been best friends for ever. Everybody looked up to them.

Sarah followed Lianne up the stairs. "And it's given me an idea . . ." Lianne carried on, opening the door of her bedroom. Lianne's room was kind of chintzy, with tied-back floral curtains and rose-pink, deep-pile carpet (the sort that gets hoovered every day). The room was large, with a big dressing-table in the corner. "Ta-da! Check this out, Sarah," Lianne said. "I've been doing it ever since I got home from the salon."

Sarah found herself looking at several sheets of paper covered with pictures cut from their favourite magazine – the one that had given Lianne the makeover. Most were 'before and after' pictures. Others were fashion shots, where Lianne had added pencilled notes, such as 'suits sallow skin', or 'adds height'. Sarah was none the wiser. "So? What is the brilliant idea, Lianne?"

"We're going to start our own makeover business!" said Lianne, tapping on the pictures with her long nails.

"What do you mean, start our own makeover business? Who do we make over? When? How?"

"It's such a great idea," said Lianne, warming to her subject. "We advertise and people come to us whenever they want and we do their hair and make them up and they look fantastic and they pay us loads of money. I know exactly how to do it, now."

It was always Lianne who had these money-making schemes – setting up a 'craft' stall (painted stones, mostly) by Sarah's house, singing carols outside the pub, selling bunches of daffodils door-to-door. And it was always Sarah who had to be practical – washing the stones before they painted them, picking the daffodils from her family's garden at five o'clock in the morning, calming the parents when they discovered their precious darlings taking money off Christmas pub-goers.

"Whoa, steady on!" said Sarah. "We can't possibly do just *any*one, *any* time. We want to be in control." She chewed on her nails for a few minutes. "I've got it! I've got it!" she announced. "We do makeovers for kids – you know, seven and eight-year-olds – and we do it like entertainers at birthday parties."

"And we can charge per head and it doesn't matter if it doesn't look very good, because they're only kids . . ." said Lianne.

"It'll have to look good or we won't get asked a second time. But if the kids look fab – which they will – we can do several parties every weekend and we'll be coining it in no time!"

"Wicked! What a team we make. We'll have to invest in new make-up and hair-styling stuff and accessories and things . . ."

"I've got a bit of money left over from my birthday . . ."

"Let's go out now."

This was what Sarah liked about Lianne. She didn't hang about.

A few weeks later, Lianne was leaning over Sarah's shoulder as she pulled the finished leaflet from the printer. "Are we cool, or what, Sarah?"

"Pretty cool."

"We're cool *and* we're going to be rich," said Lianne. "Just wait till we get these babies pinned up in all the right places."

The two of them admired their handiwork. Sarah had scanned in photos from magazines and Lianne had written the words. It was a sophisticated job. No spelling mistakes. The leaflet read:

Make your party over to

Miracle Makeovers.

Lianne and **Sarah** will *make you up*,
style your hair and let you try out
the latest in fashion.
Parties of up to ten girls, age 7-11.

Call us weekdays after 4.30 and weekends.

And then they gave Lianne's mobile number.

The clothes had been Lianne's mum's idea. She owned Little Tigers, a children's clothes shop in Cobford, so it made sense to let the girls have a few outfits that could be tried out. A businesswoman through and through, she made them put down a deposit on them first. Lianne had helped out almost full-time in the shop over the summer holidays and Sarah had made and sold lots of pairs of bead earrings to earn the money. Now they were ready to roll. The autumn term was less than a week away and the party season was about to take off.

"Stay and eat with us?" Sarah asked. There was no one at Lianne's house on a Thursday night. It was late-night shopping at Little Tigers and her dad was abroad on business.

"It depends what you're having," said Lianne, as she did every Thursday night when she stayed for supper.

"I don't know. I'll ask Mum. Or I could cook. Whatever you want, probably. We did a big Tesco's shop yesterday."

"Oh, all right then. I'll stay." Sarah couldn't remember a time when Lianne had decided not to stay. Thursday nights were part and parcel of their friendship and always had been.

The two girls walked up the long, straggly garden from the converted coach house where they'd been working. Sarah knocked on the door of the annexe where her granny lived as they passed. She pushed open the door and a small hairy dog dashed out under her feet. "Are you eating with us tonight, Granny?" she called, patting the dog.

"Millie! *Bad* dog! Come *here*!" Sarah's granny shouted after the little dog as she came to the door, a piece of sewing in her hand. "What was that, pet?"

"Supper! Are you eating with us or has Mum done you something frozen?"

"It depends what you're having, pet."

(Not you as well, thought Sarah.) "If I did some pasta, would you like that?"

"Yes please, pet. I'm always telling your mother what a good little cook you are."

Sarah looked at her watch. "OK then, Granny. Half-past seven. I'll send Lianne out to get you."

Lianne made a face and Sarah made one back.

"Make sure it's not spaghetti," said Lianne as they pushed past the Michaelmas daisies and marigolds overhanging the brick path. "I don't think I can cope with your granny eating spaghetti."

Sarah sighed. "I'll make sure it's not spaghetti," she said comfortably. Nothing ever changed. She knew how much Lianne liked eating meals round at her house. Almost anything was better than yet another microwave meal in front of the telly while her parents worked till all hours.

Ruth

Mum's still not eating, so she's sending me away. It's all settled. I'm moving to Cobford and I'm starting at a school there called King Edward's. Mum didn't give me any option. She says she's only got enough strength to look after herself and the best thing for me is to go and live with Dad and Angela and her children. At least I'll get 'a proper home life and decent meals'. More importantly, I won't feel obliged to look after her.

If I sound hacked off, it's because I am. Most teenage girls have issues with their mothers, I know, but believe me, it's a hundred times worse when your mother is sick. Just when you feel the limelight should be on you, it isn't. It's on this needy, wheedling invalid – an invalid who should be your strong, supportive, caring mother. I knew Mum couldn't help it. I saw depression and then anorexia taking her over with my own eyes. But I just wanted her to snap out of it. To smile. To eat, for God's sake. To be there for me.

Of course, as I told my best friend, Emily, it was all to do with my parents splitting up. My mum and dad had been together since they were teenagers. Then, about three years ago, Dad got completely stressed out at work and started coming home later and later, boozing till all hours with his mates, sleeping over at the office. After it had gone on for a long time, Mum finally cracked and told him he was a waste of space, totally unreliable at home, no use as a husband, father, etc. etc. and he might as well leave. Well, I didn't agree with the useless father bit, but then I didn't have any say in the matter, did I? Never mind that it tore me apart when he left and everything changed.

Mum always believed Dad loved her enough to come back. But he didn't. He stayed away. And then he met someone else, who didn't think he was useless and unreliable. Mum has her pride. She told me calmly that she'd probably married him too young. These things happen. People move on.

I go to stay with Dad and Angela at weekends quite often. He comes to pick me up. Sometimes he even fixes a few things around the house while he's here. Mum pretends that's normal. Or she used to. Before she stopped going to work. Before she stopped eating.

Well, I love my dad. I can't help it if he doesn't love Mum any more, or if she's basically been falling apart ever since he left. So I said, OK, I'll go and live with Dad and Angela. It couldn't be worse than this.

I guess I wanted to hurt her a bit. But I wasn't even going to start on the rest, like: excuse me, but where do I fit into all this? Why should I have to leave my school, leave Emily – my best friend? Move away from London, my LIFE? Live with a woman I hardly know, not to mention her son and her daughter? They'd better not mess with me at the new school, is all I can say. They'll have to take me as I am. It's not as if I want to be there. It's not as if I'd ever choose to go to a school where they wear a uniform – a stupid green uniform at that.

Dad's just arrived to pick me up. To be honest, it feels like any other time I've been to stay with him - I just have more luggage than usual. Mum handed me a big bag of clothes she'd promised me ages ago - cool eighties stuff of hers that she'd managed (I don't know how) to bring down from the attic. She hugged me harder than usual, and I felt how tiny she'd become, how like a bird.

Chapter Two

High clouds rode in a summer-blue sky; the first fallen leaves lay on the pavement, waiting to be scrunched underfoot. It was a typical first day of the new school year. Sarah watched the hordes of green-uniformed kids tramping past her house on the way to King Edward's as she waited for Lianne to pick her up. She spotted nervous Year Sevens in their over-large blazers, clutching brand new sports bags. Confident Year Eights, raucous as magpies, threw sticks up into the horse chestnut tree on the corner to knock down the conkers that weren't quite ready to fall.

Lianne had the knack of looking good in school uniform, with a whiter-than-white shirt and plenty of touches that told the world she'd look even better after four o'clock. Though Sarah looked great in anything, even a green blazer and skirt, she was usually less neat and tidy than Lianne. Today she'd been up since six-thirty straight-drying her fair hair to stop it going curly at the ends. She carried a bundle of the new flyers to drop off at a couple of shops on the way to school and to hand out to people with younger sisters.

As they turned the corner, King Edward's School – and with it the whole prospect of life as Year Nines – came into view. "Look, there's Claire!" said Lianne excitedly. "She's dyed her hair! I told her she should go blonde." Lianne loved telling people how to make the best of themselves.

"I know – doesn't it look great? Have you seen Ellie, though? She's got a terrific suntan. And she's lost weight. You said she should go on a diet, didn't you?"

"God, there's Josie. She's grosser than ever. Hide! I don't want to have to talk to her. We might be forced to listen to the next exciting instalment in the saga of her stupid swimming pool."

A group of boys a year older hung around by the gate. One of them stood slightly apart from the others. Sarah nudged Lianne and blushed. "It's Matt Johnson," she whispered.

"Didn't recognise old Zit Johnson from this distance," Lianne hissed back. "You can't see the spots from here. What's he done to *his* hair? Wo-oh, he's looking in our direction. Just keep walking." To herself, Lianne thought: so Sarah's finally let slip that she fancies someone. Now *there's* a project. This year is getting interesting already.

The noise in the corridor was deafening as the torrent of students roared down it. Like royalty, Lianne and Sarah barged confidently through the gaggles of younger kids, closely followed by Claire and Ellie and other members of their entourage. Finally the whole class burst through the doorway into the form room and scraped and clattered their way to their seats. Mr Booth, their form tutor since they'd started secondary school, took note of who was sitting with whom. Lianne-and-Sarah, queen bees as usual. Ellie and Claire at the desk next to them. Josie squashed up by the wall where it wasn't so obvious that she sat alone. All the boys at the back.

Mr Booth yelled at his class to sit down and be quiet while he took the register, and that was the new school year under way. Or so everyone thought. Until he asked Tom Cook to take the register to the secretary's office, adding that there was a new girl waiting there to join the class, so perhaps Tom could collect her at the same time.

"New girl, eh?" said Lianne to Sarah. "Perhaps she'll be cool. Perhaps she'll live near us." Making Sarah feel insecure from time to time was one of the ways Lianne hung on to her.

"She's probably really boring," said Sarah, quickly suppressing the unexpected idea that perhaps it would be quite nice to have a new friend, possibly one with an incredibly handsome older brother. "We always think new people are going to be cool and they never are." She knew that was what Lianne was really hoping. Lianne didn't want competition. Anyway, Lianne was her best friend. What was she thinking of?

Tom Cook flung open the door and made an entrance. The new girl followed him. Her green uniform was clearly brand new. The creases were still obvious. She was quite tall, with long legs. Her dark hair hung loose and straggly beyond her shoulders. It partly obscured her face, as did her glasses, but everyone could see enough to tell that she was really uncomfortable standing there.

Mr Booth clocked the empty space next to Josie and shouted, "Quiet!" again before announcing: "I'd like you all to welcome Ruth Miller who is joining us this term. I hope you'll help her to find her way around. Ruth – if you'd like to sit down by Josie over there for the moment, she'll soon make you feel at home. I'm about to give you all your timetable."

Sarah was intrigued. On first sight Ruth seemed OK – if only she didn't have to look *quite* so unenthusiastic about joining their class. Sarah watched Lianne sizing up the possible competition, like a snake assessing a small furry creature, and waited for the verdict.

"She won't make any friends if she goes round looking like she's just stepped in a pile of vomit," said Lianne. "Let's see if she's as up herself as she looks before we speak to her."

The new girl squeezed in beside Josie. She pulled a pencil case and a notebook from a velvet shoulder bag and waited to take down her timetable with the rest of the class. Lianne deliberately made a show of looking to her right before turning back to Sarah. "Check out the bag," she sniggered.

Sarah pretended to toss back her hair and checked it out. It was a great bag – quite unlike the sports bags everyone else carried and totally incongruous with the green uniform – but Sarah knew that Lianne didn't rate that sort of style at all. 'Smart' was Lianne's style. "See what you mean," she whispered back.

Ruth

We didn't wear uniform at my school in London, so any uniform sucks, but this one is green so it sucks utterly. Angela had to help me tie my tie. The other guys seem to have made an art form out of wearing school uniform, as if somewhere, deep down, they like it. They all wear their socks a certain length and have the same hairstyle – it just looks sad to me. And make-up! Some of them are plastered in it! Who's to impress at school?

This is a total nightmare. Matthew, who I suppose is a sort of stepbrother now, set off for King Edward's with me this morning and I thought, OK, maybe things won't be so bad. But then he stopped and said, no offence, but he really didn't want me to speak to him at school or let anyone know that I had anything to do with him. He asked me to walk ahead of him two roads ago. Can you believe it?

Mum rang to wish me luck this morning and I wish she hadn't. She said Emily had promised to call me tonight. I don't even want to think about how much I miss Emily. Then Angela shooed me and Matthew out of the door, not least because Maisie was building up to some sort of strop.

That's when Matthew gave me his piece about not talking to him. He just explained he had his image to keep up and he didn't want people discussing his home life, thank you very much. Sorry, and all that.

Rubbish human being that I am, it's never occurred to me that Matthew might have any problems, apart from his complexion. Nobody starving themselves to death in *his* house. He's got *my* dad, hasn't he? Maybe that's one of the problems.

He'd paused, then, to look in a shop window and do funny things to his hair, and said he'd wait while I went on ahead.

Nice to feel wanted.

I suppose all classes are the same in some respects, even on planet Cobford. I knew instantly that Josie was a total loser. It's almost like a scent someone gives off when they're so deeply unpopular. It's quite hard to tell people apart when they're all in green, but you can always spot the leaders – here they're the two girls who sit in the middle, with their hangers-on surrounding them. There's another one with bleached hair who looks quite cool. The boys are even more juvenile than our ones were. They just seem to make a lot of noise at the back of class.

When it was time to move classrooms, Josie hovered around to show me the way. I wasn't complaining though, because the layout of this school really does your head in. Once I spotted Matthew with a group of boys. It was surprisingly comforting to see a familiar face in the crowd. I smiled vaguely in his direction, before remembering his instructions, but I needn't have bothered. He blanked me completely.

I wonder what Emily's doing now? Having lunch I suppose, like I'm about to. I don't know who to sit with. Who will Emily be with today?

By the end of the day Sarah and Lianne had unloaded fifteen flyers: five in local shop windows, four pinned on school noticeboards and six handed out to schoolfriends known to have little sisters. The last of these was pressed on Matt Johnson by Lianne. (She'd spied Matt outside Little Tigers in the summer, with a woman and a small girl, so she assumed he had a younger sister.) She cornered him now, chiefly to wind Sarah up – and succeeded.

"Matt?" she called sweetly. He looked at her, looked around to see if anyone was watching, and frowned.

"What?" He kicked at an imaginary stone.

"You've got a sister, haven't you?"

"What if I have?"

"A little sister?"

"Uh huh."

Lianne had nearly faltered at this point. But only for a beat. Sarah was blushing furiously in the background – Lianne didn't want to give up now. "Here, have one of these leaflets. Your mum might be grateful to you one day." She handed him the leaflet with a smile.

Matt stuffed it in his pocket unceremoniously and walked

off with a, "Yeah, well," as Lianne ran giggling back to Sarah, now beetroot beneath her fair hair.

"What'd you do that for, Lianne? What if it works and we have to go and do makeovers at his house? I'd die, I really would!"

"You know you're longing to."

"I suppose he'd make sure he was out, wouldn't he?" Sarah tried to console herself. "He's not the sort to stay around for his little sister's birthday party, is he?"

"Exactly. Ooh look, there's Josie with her new best friend." It was clear even from this distance that Ruth was trying to lose Josie before walking home. "So that's the new girl fixed up, then."

"Poor her," said Sarah, but Lianne wasn't listening.

Ruth

Angela was really sweet to me when I got home from school. I still think of her as Dad's girlfriend, but if Matthew's a sort of stepbrother, that makes her almost a stepmother. (And Maisie my stepsister – not a pleasant thought.) Angela had a pot of tea and some brownies waiting. When did Mum ever do that? She even asked if I'd prefer to have it in front of the TV. Matthew walked in soon after me. "Don't expect this every day," he said, laughing, all normal again as he grabbed a couple of brownies. "Thanks, Ma. Ruth can stay!"

I felt like saying, "Oh, so you've stopped blanking me now, have you?" But I didn't want to dump him in it. I was just glad that we were still speaking. He disappeared with his tea and the brownies.

"So, how was it? Did Matthew help you find your way about? It's no fun being the new girl, is it?"

"Huh. Well. Yeah, OK, not too bad," I mumbled, not quite committing myself. I'm trying to understand Matthew's position here, believe me. I don't know how I'd feel if it was the other way round. Maybe, if he didn't have such silly hair, I'd be proud of him and want my friends to know that we were a bit related. Which must mean he's not proud enough of me. Perhaps I'm a total embarrassment to him. Ah well.

After school Lianne left Sarah at her house. "Got to get home," said Lianne. "Dad's due home from the States today. Big deal. He likes me to be right there, so we can be one smiling, happy family." She sighed and then pulled herself together. "See ya."

Sarah went in the back way. It was still sunny and Granny was sitting outside with her sewing. Millie lay at her feet. "Hi, Granny." Sarah threw her bag on the grass. "Who else is home?"

"Well, your father and Ben are doing something on the computer in the coach house and your mother's collecting the little ones. How was your first day back?"

"OK." Sarah sat on the sunny patch of ground with Millie and stroked her ears. "Granny, people grow out of spots, don't they?"

"Of course they do. It's just all those hormones rushing around. I don't know why you're worrying, pet. You've got a lovely clear skin!"

Sarah smiled. She plucked some grass and scattered it before changing the subject. "We've got a new girl in our class."

"That's nice, pet. Maybe you should bring her back here to play."

"We don't *play* any more, Granny."

"Well, whatever it is you do. She'll need some friends. It's horrible being the new girl. I had to move all over the place during the War, you know, and I hated it."

"Maybe, Granny," said Sarah, and rolled over on the grass with Millie. It was the person underneath the spots that she liked, anyway. And the nice eyes.

Ruth

Emily just rang. It was so great to talk to her, but now I feel so homesick – school-sick, friend-sick, whatever – that I almost wish she hadn't.

This is how it went:

"Roo!"

"Ems!"

"How you doin'? How's the gorgeous green uniform, you sad woman! Have you made any new friends as nice as me?"

"Of course! It was love at first sight. Her name's Josie and she hasn't got any other friends, so she just adores me!"

I could hear Emily worrying. "Well, that's cool. Great," she said in a small voice.

"Gotcha!" I shouted down the phone. "She's the class reject. Anyway, I feel like they're all from a different planet. They look kind of natty in their uniforms and they do odd things with their hair and they wear loads of slap. You should see them, Em. They're just not like you and me."

"No one is like you and me. Now, do you want to hear about my lonely old day, or not?"

And Em had missed me like I'd missed her. It must be harder for her in some ways because everything else is the same. We'd been a pair, just like those stupid girls in my class at King Edward's. Except that we weren't stupid. So Em didn't have me to sit with, walk to classes with, have lunch with, go home with…

"Come back," she pleaded. "You could live with us. You know Mum offered." I knew she had. But my mum wasn't having any of it. She said that Dad needed to do his share. She didn't want him let off the hook. She wanted Angela to be put out. "So when are you coming back for the weekend?" Emily asked after she'd been silent for a moment.

"I don't know. Dad and Angela seem to think it's best if I don't go home for a bit, not before I've settled in."

"What about me? I need to see you."

"Tell you what. It's Maisie's eighth birthday quite soon and I don't want to be here for that. It's not as if she's my real little sister." I lowered my voice, even though no one was around. "She's a bit of a spoiled brat – gets everything she wants and whinges if she doesn't. Angela's getting an entertainer in, so I won't be needed to help or anything."

"Do you remember my eighth birthday party?" Emily asked. "We got the giggles so badly we wet our knickers – both of us?"

"How could I ever forget?" I said. "Someone told the boys, didn't they? And they wouldn't sit next to us for weeks in case we did it again."

"Anyway!" Em almost yelled. "Come that weekend, then. Mum's going on at me to get off the phone because supper's on the table. Hey – you can email me now! I've got my own computer…" But she said she'd have to tell me next time because she really really had to go. I heard her mother barking, "Emily! Now!" in the background, so I knew she had to. That's all right. I like Emily's mum. She's normal.

While Ruth was on the phone to Emily, Matthew was behind the locked bathroom door peering into the mirror.

He was a good-looking boy with thick dark hair, but all he could see reflected was the acne that plagued him and always flared up at the worst possible moment. Was it calming down, just a little, with the new homeopathic remedy?

Matthew pondered his situation. He was used to Ruth coming for the odd weekend. She didn't interfere. She was sort of family by now. But the thought of having her living in his house 24/7 and going to his school – that was a tough one.

At King Edward's Matthew had friends, but they were merciless about his skin – Pizza Face! Spotty! Zit Johnson! One big joke, he was. That was how those two girls had made him feel today, trying to wind him up.

And now, with Ruth here to stay, he couldn't escape the torment even at home. What secrets concerning the private life of Zit Johnson might she divulge? It must never happen. Better to keep everything separate. Ruth seemed to understand.

Chapter Three

On Friday after school, as Lianne and Sarah walked home, Lianne's mobile started to chirrup. They weren't allowed to bring mobiles into school, but petty rules like that didn't concern Lianne. The annoying little tune went on relentlessly. "Hell, where is it?" she asked, scrabbling frantically through her bag.

Sarah dipped into Lianne's blazer pocket. "Here, idiot."

"Hello?" said Lianne breathlessly. "Damn! They've rung off."

"Probably your mum saying she'll be late. Check the number."

"I don't recognise it."

"Ring it back then. Maybe it's a boy who fancies you."

"Oh, sure." Lianne rang the number back. She suddenly snapped into business mode. "It's Lianne Bartlett speaking . . . Miracle Makeovers, yes . . . Definitely . . . Saturday week? Definitely. We'll come and see you this weekend, then. Sunday 5 o'clock. Definitely. Bye."

"*Definitely*!" said Sarah, mimicking.

"You may laugh," said Lianne. "We have a gig! Don't talk – I've got to write down the address while I remember." She pulled her rough book and a pencil from her bag.

"Weyhey! Tell me more."

Lianne finished scribbling. "Now. Marquess Drive. It's over near that little shopping parade, I think. Other side of the railway bridge. Nine-year-old's birthday party. Ten girls, the woman said. That means they might have to take it in turns to wear the clothes. Let's hope someone's got a camera."

They stopped outside Sarah's house. The first weekend of term suddenly seemed full of promise. "We'd better practise," said Sarah. "Loads. We don't want to mess it up."

"Can I come over tomorrow?" said Lianne. "Not too early. I want to sleep in. And I don't want to work in the shop, so I need a good excuse. You could practise on your little sister tonight."

"Poor Bronnie. She's only four!" said Sarah.

"She'll be perfect," said Lianne. "Eight and nine-year-olds can't be any worse."

Ruth

Thank God it's the weekend now. I can wear comfortable clothes. Matthew can take a break from blanking me. I can chill out in my room. It will never feel like my room, but it's not bad. In fact, it's not a bad house. Not like ours, though. It's all Angela's furniture and taste apart from Dad's study, which is crammed with piles of his stuff – books, CDs, notebooks, photo albums. You can hardly squeeze in the door, but I like it in there – it reminds me of being little.

I must get Dad to set me up so I can email Emily. That'll be cool. There's so much to tell her. I don't seem to have made any new friends – apart from Josie of course, so that should please Em. It's very hard to like Josie. She makes it harder by boasting about their posh house and three cars and half a swimming pool (it's still being built) and the uncle who's been on TV. For some reason, the two popular girls, Lianne and Sarah, have decided to blank me. Which means the others all follow suit. Not pleasant. I'm not used to being treated as a loser.

At home Angela is still cool. Maisie is still a pain. You'd think it might be fun to have a little sister, wouldn't you? But not Maisie. And you'd certainly think it might be fun to have an older brother. But not Matthew! He speaks to me in the house, but as soon as we're out of that door he doesn't want to know. I wondered if his problem was something to do with school, but I haven't dared get close enough to find out. I don't understand boys.

On Sunday Lianne and Sarah both failed to persuade their parents to drive them to Marquess Drive, the home of their first client. They set off on the half-hour walk at four-fifteen in a cloudburst, which didn't put them in the best of tempers, especially as they'd decided to wear their most professional-looking clothes and high-heeled shoes. They wheeled their gear, including the Little Tiger clothes, in two smart little suitcases.

"What *do* we look like?" said Sarah, trying to keep cheerful as they splashed through the puddles in the uneven pavements, ruining the shoes that were already killing their feet. "I'm going to take off my shoes and go barefoot. It couldn't be worse!"

"We must look as if we're running away!" said Lianne. "I hope these suitcases are waterproof."

"We were daft to bring everything with us today."

"Well, we won't make that mistake again." Lianne looked grim.

"Fifteen more minutes at the most," said Sarah. They trudged on.

Marquess Drive was a close like the one Lianne lived in. Chintzy. Number 4 was smartly painted, with orderly flowerbeds in the front garden. A small pink bicycle was propped up in the porch. They hastily put on their tight wet shoes and Lianne rang the doorbell.

Mrs Plumley opened the door. "Goodness gracious!" she said, eyeing the two drowned rats that had fetched up on her doorstep. "You'd better come in. I was expecting someone older," she added, as they followed her into the big kitchen. She took their dripping jackets and hung them over the backs of chairs. "You're rather late, so we don't have long. Sit down and tell me what you do."

"How did you get hold of us, Mrs Plumley?" asked Sarah politely, while Lianne opened the cases.

"A friend of mine. Angela Johnson. Her son brought your flyer home from school. I presume you know him."

Lianne answered quickly before Sarah had a chance to faint and said, "Matt? Oh yes, he's a great friend of ours."

"If Jessica's party is a success, Angela will ask you along to her daughter Maisie's party, which is a couple of weeks after. Jessica's older than Maisie, so it won't be the same children. Now, how much do you charge?"

Sarah was still sitting with her mouth open at the thought of going into Matt Johnson's house, so Lianne replied, "Fifty pounds all in – which works out at five pounds a head," she said. "And a ten per cent discount in Little Tigers clothes shop if they want to buy the clothes for themselves."

"That sounds reasonable," said Mrs Plumley. "How do you propose to organise ten little girls?"

"Oh, that's no problem," said Sarah, coming back to life.

"I'm used to children. We'll just divide them into two groups and Lianne and I will do five each. The others can watch."

"We'll be relying on the pair of you to keep everyone occupied. Are you sure you can cope?" Mrs Plumley glanced at the clock.

"It'll be fine," said Lianne reassuringly. "Now, these are the clothes" – she held some of them up – "and this is the make-up and hair stuff."

"Very nice, very nice. I'm sure Jessica will love them," said Mrs Plumley, brushing the clothes aside and standing up. "I have to pick Jessica up now. I'll see you next Saturday. The party begins at three-thirty, so you'd better be here by three to set up."

Lianne stuffed everything back into the cases and the girls took their jackets, still wet, from Mrs Plumley as she opened the door for them. "Goodbye," she called, shutting the door quickly and leaving them in the porch.

"Phew, " said Sarah as she struggled into her jacket. "She really didn't want to know, did she? I thought we'd at least meet the famous Jessica. I'm not sure what nine-year-olds are like these days."

"Piece of cake," said Lianne, stepping into a puddle that came up to her ankles. "I didn't mind her being businesslike. She must have realised straight away how professional we are. And we'll make fifty quid! Yay!"

Ruth

From ruth@yes.com
Sunday night
Hi Ems!

Ta-da! Dad's set me up on his computer, so HELLOOO!

I'm a bit more cheerful now than I was when you rang last week. The weekend's been OK because I like being with Dad and he likes being with me. We've spent a lot of time on the computer and listening to CDs and watching TV and stuff. And he's put up shelves in my room and found a CD player for me to have in there. He's even trying to get me a second-hand computer. He says Matthew has one for homework and he doesn't see why I shouldn't have one as well. Then I'll be able to email you from the privacy of my own room. A mobile would be good, but we're not allowed them at school and I don't want to ask Dad for too much all at once. I'd forgotten how much I've been missing him. Daft, isn't it? Life would be so much simpler if parents didn't split up.

Now, about me coming home to see you . . . I'd like to stay with you rather than actually go home, but I'm not sure how to play that one with Mum, so I need a bit of time to think it over. Maisie's birthday is in three weeks' time, so that's the date. She's getting excited already because she thinks she's having a 'makeover' party. Someone comes in and makes them up and does their hair and they get to try on trendy clothes. Sounds revolting to me. Whatever happened to Pass the Parcel and Musical Bumps? Anyway, it might not happen. One of Angela's friends is trying the makeover people out next weekend. I sort of hope it does work out with them because then I won't feel I ought to be helping. I mean, I don't, but you know how it is. So put it in your diary. We're on.

Chapter Four

"Tell your little sister to sit still, Sarah."

"Owww," wailed Bronwen. "It's itchy."

"Come on, Bronnie. You know we need to practise. Don't you like this nice foundation?"

"No," said Bronwen, looking at herself in the mirror. "It's making my face all red."

"Stop complaining, Bronwen," said Lianne. "You're lucky. The kids at our makeover parties pay to have this done to them."

"Actually, Lianne," said Sarah, "she's right. I think you'd better wipe that stuff off and get on with the eye make-up. I think she's having an allergic reaction to it or something."

"Better her than someone who's paying for it," said Lianne, dabbing sharply at Bronwen's face with cotton wool.

"There, there, Bronnie," said Sarah soothingly to compensate for Lianne's jabbing hands and long fingernails. The skin was looking very angry and red. Sarah handed her little sister a face flannel soaked in cold water. "Just don't tell Mum, OK?"

*

"What's up with Bronwen?" asked Sarah's mother, looking into the front room where Bronnie sat quietly in front of the television.

"She's fine. Can I help you unpack the shopping?" said Sarah innocently.

"I'll help too," said Lianne, who was staying for Thursday supper as usual. "Ooh – pizzas! Are they for tonight?"

Before long, Sarah's whole family was crammed into the kitchen – her parents, Granny, Ben, and her eight-year-old brother Freddie. Only Bronwen hadn't put in an appearance.

"Come on, Bronnie!" called Sarah's father. "Pizza! Your favourite. I can't believe you're really interested in watching the news!"

"I don't want her watching the news," said Sarah's mother. "She's too young for war and starvation. I thought you two girls were going to look after her, not just stick her in front of the telly."

"We did," said Sarah. "So well, in fact, that she's tired out."

"And her face is all red," added Freddie.

By now everyone was digging into their pizzas. Bronwen couldn't resist the smell any longer and drifted in, still clutching the flannel to her face.

"Goodness, Bronnie!" said Sarah's mother, looking closely at her. "Freddie's right. Your face is all red. And lumpy."

"It's probably the foundation we used," said Lianne, matter-of-factly.

"I *beg* your pardon?" said Sarah's mother. "Bronwen – what has your big sister been doing to you?"

"They've been practising makeovers," said Bronnie.

"Where's my pizza?"

"Didn't you know, Mum? They've been doing it all week," said Ben helpfully.

"Sarah!" said her mother reproachfully.

"Well, we weren't to know she'd be allergic to something," said Sarah. "She's been fine every other day this week. It was just today. We thought we'd get to grips with her skin, rather than just her eyes and lips."

"Yeah, we're brilliant on eyes and lips now," said Lianne.

"Honestly, you two," said Sarah's mother. "You're obsessed. You're losing touch with reality." She looked at Bronwen's lumpy cheeks. "It seems to be calming down, now, thank goodness. The cold flannel was a good idea."

"We won't use that foundation again," said Lianne.

"You don't get it, do you?" Sarah's mother addressed her daughter, but she was really speaking to Lianne. She sometimes worried about Sarah's best friend. Once that girl got the bit between her teeth there really was no stopping her. "Bronwen is four years old. She doesn't need a makeover! Any more than any other little kid, as far as I can see."

"Oh, Mum," said Sarah, disappointed, "I thought you approved of our Miracle Makeovers idea."

"I'm having second thoughts." Sarah's mother sighed. "I mean, I can't bear the idea of kids wanting to look like teenagers when they're barely out of nappies. But I suppose if they enjoy it . . . "

"It's no worse than dressing up, dear," said Granny to Sarah's mum. "And I never could keep you out of my make-up box!"

"I like having makeovers," said Bronnie, joining in. "I like Lianne making me pretty."

"See?" said Lianne.

Ruth

I've been at King Edward's over a week now. It's Thursday already and weekend number two is in sight. I feel as if this is all some dream I'm living in, and that I'll wake up and go back to my own life any minute. Someone else's mum gives me breakfast. A stranger in a green uniform looks back at me from the mirror. Someone else's brother makes me walk ahead of him in the morning. I go into someone else's school with someone else's teachers. The only thing is, I don't have someone else's friends. I don't have any friends to speak of. I have nerdy Josie who follows me around like a pathetic puppy. I'll give her this – she's very persistent. She won't let go. I've even had to refuse an offer to see her half-built swimming pool this weekend.

I didn't think I was that unappealing. I really don't under-stand why none of these boring people wants to be my friend – someone other than Josie, that is. The boys are just as bad. Do I look like an alien or something? Is it the fact that I don't scrape my hair back into a ponytail? I mean, I don't know what everyone sees in Lianne and Sarah – they're always in a huddle about something, always giggling. (Bit like Em and me used to be, if I'm honest.) But I'd at least like them to talk to me or be a teensy bit friendly. Ellie and Claire don't seem quite as bad, but they've got each other – and they've been brainwashed by the other two, like all the rest of the class.

I must email Emily tonight.

The day before the first makeover party, Lianne called for Sarah as usual. "What's Bronnie's face like today?" she asked.

"Still a bit pink, but no lumps," said Sarah. "Mum's not happy."

"Do you think it was the foundation?"

"I'm sure it was. Mum must've had it for ten years at least. Everything we've bought is hypo-allergenic."

"Did you tell her we'd borrowed it?"

"What do you think?"

The two girls turned in through the school gate, where they ran in to Ellie and Claire.

Ruth Miller hung around, smiling vaguely, but Lianne was already regaling Claire and Ellie with the latest on Bronnie's face, so they ignored her as usual. Ruth was pounced on anyway by Josie, who insisted on keeping her up to speed with the swimming pool saga.

"You'll never guess what," said Josie breathlessly.

"What?" Ruth obliged, watching the four girls turn their backs on her. Unhappily, Ruth hitched her velvet bag over her shoulder and resigned herself to being told about expensive little tiles that had an uncanny knack of coming unstuck.

"What do you think of her, anyway?" Ellie asked Lianne, nodding in the direction of Ruth.

"Speccy four-eyes over there? Bit stuck up, if you ask me," said Lianne.

"Where does she live?" said Claire.

"Dunno. She comes over the railway bridge."

"On foot?"

"Must do. Anyway, you don't want to worry about her. She's got a nice pal – Josie."

"Poor thing," said Sarah.

Lianne heard her this time. "Excuse me?" she said. "You haven't exactly been rushing to make friends."

"It does seem . . . she does seem quite . . . self-contained," said Sarah. "It's not as if she hangs around with us, is it?"

"Stuck up. As I said," said Lianne.

Sarah glanced over at Ruth and Josie, and caught Ruth's wistful look. Sarah turned back to the group, where Lianne was suggesting that they did a makeover on Freddie tonight.

By Saturday morning Miracle Makeovers was ready to run. Lianne arrived at Sarah's house for eleven o'clock. Sarah's dad had been dragooned into giving them a lift to Marquess Drive; Lianne's dad would do it next time – if he was around.

"I think that's cheating," said Ben. "You ought at least to pay for a cab out of these massive earnings."

"Next week, dear boy," said Lianne. "Next week, when we'll be rich – RICH!"

By lunch time the girls had packed and repacked the clothes in their little cases a dozen times. Freddie, Bronwen and even Sarah's mother had been made up several times over. Foundation had been dropped from the make-up box and replaced with glitter gel. Bronwen and Freddie both had coloured streaks in their hair.

Sarah and Lianne hardly touched the soup and sand-wiches they were offered for lunch. By two o'clock they had changed their own outfits at least three times and styled each other's hair. "Maybe we shouldn't be smart," said Sarah. "Maybe comfortable is better around little kids."

"No. We need to set a good example," said Lianne. "We need to be trendy. To have a look these kids want to emulate."

"Oh. OK," said Sarah, silenced by Lianne's long words. "Trendy it is, then."

Lianne looked at her watch. "Two-fifteen. Only half an

hour before we leave. Let's make sure we've got everything. You go through the list and I'll say if it's there."

"For the twenty-third time," said Sarah.

Twenty helium balloons proclaiming '9 years old today' bobbed above the front gate of 4 Marquess Drive. Halfway up the garden path was a banner saying 'Happy Birthday, Jessica'. Bunting fluttered across the front of the house.

It had started to rain again on the way there, but now the sky was clear and the garden looked bright and autumnal. Lianne and Sarah ducked under the banner with their cases. Mrs Plumley opened the front door before they could ring and two girls danced out, shrieking, "They're here! They're here!" One pulled on the handle of Lianne's suitcase and dragged her in the door.

"Gently, girls," called Mrs Plumley. "They're very excited, I'm afraid," she said to Sarah. "Come through. We thought we'd set you up in the garden."

Sarah looked at Jessica and her friend. It was obvious which one was Jessica because she was a miniature version of her mother. What's more, she was tall for her age. Her hair was pulled into a topknot, rather like Sarah's own. It was even held in place with silk flower clips, as Sarah's was. She wore a sparkly top and jeans very like the ones Lianne had been provided with by the makeover people. She looked about thirteen. So did her friend.

"Help!" whispered Sarah, as they were frogmarched into the garden. "How can we give these kids a makeover? They don't need one!'

"Everyone can use a makeover," said Lianne. "Relax! It's going to be fine." Then her kitten heels sank into the sodden lawn.

Sarah's heels went the same way. She looked up at the sky. The brightness had been short-lived. Ominous-looking clouds loured back at her. A table had been set up with a big piece of paper sellotaped to the front. 'Makeovers here!' was written on it in large blue felt-tip letters. It didn't look promising. A single plump raindrop fell on the paper and the M in Makeovers started to run.

Mrs Plumley followed them out. "Nothing to worry about!" she said cheerily. "The weather forecast is good for this afternoon. I'll leave you two to set up. Come along, girls, I need some help putting candles on the cake."

A gust of wind ripped one side of the paper away from the table. Lianne swore. "What does she mean, set up? One table! No chairs!"

"We've got to be positive," said Sarah. "Now, what do you reckon? Two queues of five? Should we do clothes-clothes-clothes, make-up-make-up-make-up, hair-hair-hair, sort of thing, or five complete makeovers?"

"Clothes first," said Lianne. "No. Hair."

"Well, I was thinking make-up first," said Sarah. "Those two have pretty cool hair and clothes, but I don't think they're wearing make-up."

"Oooh," wailed Lianne. "Why didn't we think about this before?"

"Because *you* were too keen on practising make-up."

"Well, *you* needed the practice," Lianne retorted.

"That's not true!" said Sarah. "I'm just as good at make-up as you are!"

Lianne opened her mouth to argue some more, but Jessica and her friend came bowling out into the garden at that point. "Oh," said Jessica. "I thought it would all be ready by now. Everyone will be here soon."

Sarah took charge, as she usually did to make Lianne's brainwaves work. "We need two chairs, Jessica. For people to sit on while we do their faces and hair. And – " Sarah looked around the garden in despair – "We really need somewhere to put the clothes. Normally," she lied, "we'd lay them out on a sofa or something."

Jessica narrowed her eyes at Sarah and looked unwilling to help. "I can't carry stuff," she said. "I might spoil my outfit." And then the doorbell rang. "Come on, Sophie," she said. "This might be the boys!"

"Boys?" Lianne's jaw dropped. "Nobody said anything about boys! Can this get any worse?"

It started to rain in earnest. "Yes," said Sarah. "Much worse."

The one good thing about the rain was that it allowed Miracle Makeovers to work indoors. There were indeed ten little girls, but there were also two little boys. And 'little' is relative. Some of these eight- and-nine-year olds were practically teenagers. They certainly dressed like them. Lianne and Sarah laid the clothes over the back of the settee, which the children – including the boys – took as an invitation to try them on. Chaos ensued as the boys pulled little tops on and the girls fought over who wanted to wear what. Jessica, aware that it was her birthday party going pear-shaped, became very bossy. She shrieked at the others to get in line and stamped her foot when they wouldn't do as they were told.

Mrs Plumley tried to calm things down by setting up a video for those who were waiting, but then the girls who were being made up insisted on twisting round to watch it. The noise level was horrendous, made worse by the children yelling at each other to keep quiet. Lianne was working on the make-up-make-up-makeup, hair-hair-hair principle while Sarah had gone for the make-up-hair-clothes routine, so the kids in each of their queues were jealous of one another.

It was a nightmare. By teatime Lianne had made up four of her five girls and Sarah had done complete makeovers on two of hers. The boys were dressed in the remainder of the clothes and sat down to eat in them.

Lianne was having none of it. "You can get those clothes off right now!" she shouted, tired and furious.

"Neh, neh, neh!" they teased, mimicking her tone of voice precisely, and ran out into the muddy garden, clutching greasy burgers.

"I'll make you pay for those clothes if you spoil them!" yelled Lianne, wagging a long-nailed finger at the culprits.

Sarah ran after her. "It's OK, Lianne," she said. "They're only having fun. Aren't you, boys?"

"Whose side are you on?" Lianne was practically in tears. "We spent the entire summer holidays earning those clothes!"

"Lianne, Lianne." Sarah cornered her in the garden. "Hey. Chill. These kids are here to enjoy themselves. We'll never be asked again if we lose it and the guests hate every minute. It's a steep learning curve, as they say. We've got to learn from it." She stroked Lianne's arm.

"OK, OK," said Lianne, shaking her off. She looked down at her pale trousers all splattered with mud and winced at Sarah. "From now on, it's fun-fun-fun!"

After tea, the kids who'd been made over were keen to see what would happen to their friends. The girls nagged the boys out of the Little Tigers clothes and Jessica's dad had the sense to take them outside to play football. Sarah's fourth victim happened to be a neighbour who was younger than Jessica – a little sweetheart called Megan, who'd arrived in her big sister's outgrown party dress and loved every second of her makeover. Her enthusiasm infected the others who gathered around to see what Sarah would do to her.

Meanwhile, Lianne had finished doing make-up and had moved on to hair, where she was in her element – twisting, plaiting and spraying like a professional. She leaned over to Sarah and whispered, "Hey – this ain't so bad!"

"Only forty minutes to go," Sarah whispered back. "I hope Dad isn't late."

"I really like these clothes," said Megan. "Can I keep them?"

"I wish you could," said Sarah, "but we have to take them for other little girls to try on at other birthday parties."

"Ooh!" said Megan. "Are you the people who are going to do my friend Maisie's party?"

"Is that Maisie Johnson?"

"Yes – she's going to be eight. We're in the same class at school."

Lianne, ever alert to anything to do with the Johnsons now Sarah was interested in Matt, was eavesdropping. "Yes, that's right. Especially if you remember to tell her how brilliant we are."

"And does that mean I can try on the clothes again?"

"Definitely," said Sarah, wishing she'd never let on to Lianne about Matt Johnson in the first place.

Ruth

From ruth@yes.com
28/9 17.00 hrs
Hi Emily!

I'm typing this on my very own computer in my room. How cool is that? I'm glad I've got it, because I'm quite bored this weekend. Dad set me up with this and then he had to go off and do some work. Matthew's gone to stay over with a friend and Angela's taken Maisie out to buy some new shoes and get some ideas for her birthday present. I so wish I was in London with you, wandering down the Broadway, bumping into friends, thinking about going into town tonight (and never getting our act together to actually do it). I don't know what people do on a Saturday night here. I mean, Josie's probably stuffing her face at Pizza Hut with her rich uncle – but Sarah and Lianne might just have something going. With Ellie and Claire perhaps. I'll have to ask Matthew where people go – but you can guess what he'll say! "Yeah, I go to this really cool place with shedloads of popular people, but just don't come with me, OK? Or I might have to introduce you and that would kill me" sort of thing.

I will definitely come and see you in (LESS THAN) TWO WEEKS! Not next weekend, but the one after. I'll talk to Dad about it. And I'll tell him I'm staying with you. I still can't decide whether to tell Mum.

Love ya,

R

By the time Lianne and Sarah got home they were completely shattered. Mrs Plumley had tried to pay them less because of the mayhem, but Lianne had stood her ground bravely. "I really don't think that's fair, Mrs Plumley. You said there were going to be ten children and there were twelve. No one warned us that there would be boys, either. In fact, we should probably be charging more, because they've got mud on some of the clothes."

Sarah had looked on in admiration as Mrs Plumley caved in. "Well. All right. I suppose so. But don't expect any recommendations from me. I was hoping for something rather more professional."

Now they sat with their feet up in front of the television, the muddy clothes whirring round in the washing machine. "Thank goodness it's all over," said Sarah. "Do you think she meant what she said about not recommending us? I'm not sure that I could bear to go through all that again, anyway."

"Cow," said Lianne again, crunching her way through a packet of Hula Hoops. "After all we did."

"I suppose if we were better organised . . . That little girl Megan enjoyed it, didn't she?"

"They all enjoyed it." Lianne seemed to have forgotten the disastrous bits already. "And Megan is Maisie Johnson's friend, remember. She'll recommend us and if Maisie's mum's got any sense, she'll take far more notice of her than the pathetic Mrs Plumley. I know my mum would. So, there you are, then: Matt Johnson, here we come!"

"Don't say that. I don't want even to think about it being Matt's house. It's not as if he's going to be there, is it? And anyway, it probably won't happen. And I'm not sure I like him any more anyway."

Lianne wasn't going to let her get away with that. "Course you do. You *lurve* him!"

"I do not!"

Lianne stood up, laughing, "Have it your own way!" She

headed for the kitchen. "When will your folks be back?"

"Late, Dad said. They're taking Granny over to Uncle Bill's and staying on for supper."

"Excellent." Lianne was fossicking around in the freezer. "We can eat these pasta bakes, can't we?"

"Go for it. Make sure you get the microwave timing right. I'll look for that DVD. And that's our Saturday night sorted, isn't it?"

While Sarah and Lianne were watching a DVD and Ruth was downloading music with her dad, Matthew was spending his Saturday night hanging out with his friends near the library. It was in a triangle with a pub and an off-licence and a video shop, so there were plenty of people to annoy while they shared some cider in a Coke bottle and smoked cigarettes. There weren't any girls there, although, along with football and computer games and money-making scams, they were discussed avidly, especially the better-looking ones in the year below. Someone mentioned the new girl in the same class as the awesome Lianne Bartlett and Sarah Gray, and Matthew congratulated himself on having managed to keep their connection a secret.

Chapter Five

Ruth

Mum sounded terrible on the phone last night. Her voice was all wobbly and she kept doing nervous little coughs. I think the lonely weekend got to her. She said how much she'd missed me. I asked her if she'd been eating properly and she said she'd had a bit of this and that, so I know she hasn't. I talked to Dad about it, but he wasn't a whole lot of help. "I feel I ought to be there," I said. "She needs someone there to remind her to eat." "Not your job," he told me. "You've got a life to lead and a new school to get used to. I do wish she wouldn't do this to you." So it went on. Dad doesn't really want to think about Mum. It makes him feel guilty, though he's always telling me it takes two to break up a marriage.

I felt pretty terrible too, this morning, as I tied my vile green tie and frowned at myself in the mirror. I feel as though I'm in limbo. There's a whole new life here that I don't want and a whole old life that I miss so much it kills me. I can't bear being so far down the social ladder at King Edward's, especially when stupid cows like Lianne are at the top of it. It really hurts. At my old school Emily and I were the cool ones.

Angela and Matthew were having an argument at breakfast. It was something to do with her going through his pockets, I think. Well, that would annoy anyone, but Matthew's so darned sensitive about his privacy all the time. Anyway, he stormed off to school without waiting for me. When I caught up with him, which I didn't do on purpose, he was practically at the school gate. I said, "What am I supposed to do now? Follow you or go on ahead?"

"I don't care either way," he said. He was frantic. "But I don't want anyone to see you talking to me. OK?" Which made me feel just great, especially after a weekend of relative normality.

When Josie lay in wait for me and started going on about her stupid swimming pool all over again, I bit her head off. "Shut up, Josie!" I said, "I am SO not interested," and then ran away like a coward when I saw her face crumple.

"I've just seen the new girl mouthing off at Josie," said Claire, with some satisfaction. "And then she legged it. Look, she's lurking over there."

The other three turned to look. Ruth was standing with her head bent, scuffing the ground with her foot. Lianne carried on trying to tell Claire and Ellie about their first makeover party, but Claire was getting fidgety. "And something else," she said. "I saw her talking to Zit Johnson on the way here." That stopped Lianne in her tracks.

Sarah felt herself blushing at the mere mention of Matt's name. "'Talking' talking?" asked Lianne, "Or just 'I'm a stuck-up cow and you're in my way' talking?"

Claire thought about this. "Dunno," she said. "He seemed quite narky with her."

"That's what we like," said Lianne. "She probably whacked him with her crusty bag."

Still recovering from her embarrassment, Sarah suddenly spoke out, "I don't know why you're all so mean about her. She hasn't done anything to hurt us."

"She's hurting you if she's making moves on Matt Johnson," said Lianne sharply.

"Thank *you*, Lianne," said Sarah. "Tell the world, why don't you?"

"Ooh," said Claire. "Has Sarah got the hots for Zit Johnson then?"

"Shut up, all of you," said Sarah, and marched off.

"Hmm. What an interesting morning this is turning out to be," said Claire, and the three of them sauntered towards the door in Sarah's wake.

Lianne could be ruthless. Sarah knew that. Sometimes it was funny, but today it wasn't. And somehow it was always just after she and Lianne had been particularly close – like at the makeover party – that Lianne seemed to turn on her, as if she couldn't quite cope with that closeness, wanted to dent it a bit. As Sarah sat in her place in the classroom, waiting for Lianne to join her, she was appalled to see her march up to Ruth.

Lianne was smiling a dangerous smile. "So you know Matt Johnson?" she asked Ruth.

Ruth looked up and adjusted her glasses. "No," she said cautiously. Then, "Who's he?" she added.

"Just some plonker in the year above us," said Lianne. "Claire said you were talking to him."

"Must've been someone else," said Ruth, starting to root around in her bag.

Mr Booth swept into the classroom. "Settle down now," he said, and anyone looking in Ruth's direction would have seen her expression of sheer relief as Lianne hurried back to her seat.

Ruth

From ruth@yes.com

Hi Emily

Just had the day from hell. Let me out! I wanna come home!

Matthew had a row with Angela this morning and took it out on me. I took it out on Josie, which made me feel mean. Then Lianne, the mouthy one of the two girls I told you about, suddenly came up and asked me if I knew Matthew – completely out of the blue. I pretended I didn't and I think I got away with it, but I can't think why they should care in the first place. I tell you, I'm dead if Matthew finds out they're asking about him. Crazy, but that's the way it is with him. And I do sort of understand.

When I got home, Maisie was getting all overexcited and uppity about her birthday. She's desperate to have a Makeover party, but Angela isn't sure because her friend tried out the girls who do it and said they weren't very good. Lots of pouting and shouting and sulking and Angela saying she'll think about it. Dad comes home and doesn't want to be involved – not his daughter etc, etc. And you can imagine how that went down. Then Matthew, still cross with Angela for going through his pockets, saying the girls who do the makeovers go to his school and NO WAY are they coming to his house and then I lost it too and screamed at them all – wasn't it bad enough for me having to stay with them without them all arguing all the time, and Dad tries to protect me and Angela gets huffy ... AAARGH. It's a NIGHTMARE!!!!

"Sarah? Guess what!"

"What? Hurry up, Lianne. There's something I don't want to miss on the telly."

"I just got a call from Mrs Johnson!"

"You never!"

"She wants us to go over after school tomorrow!"

"I'll die!"

Sarah and Lianne stood outside the Johnsons' house the following evening. Sarah was in danger of bottling out. "What will we do if Matt's there?"

"Behave normally, of course! Get a grip, Sarah. There's money in this."

"But –"

"No buts." Lianne marched up to the front door. As she rang the doorbell she turned back to Sarah. "And possibly *romance* in it – for you – too."

Sarah was practically hyperventilating by the time Angela Johnson opened the door. A little girl pushed forward. "Are you the people who are going to do my makeover party?"

"Hush, Maisie," said Angela. "Nothing's definite yet. Hello, girls. Come into the kitchen. Tea?"

"Yes, please," said Lianne.

"No, thanks," said Sarah, glaring at Lianne.

"Sell yourselves to me," said Angela. "Maisie's very keen to have you, so I'll be quite easily persuaded."

"The thing is," said Lianne, "you don't have to listen to what Mrs Plumley says. As long as we have enough time to set ourselves up, we'll be fine. And we don't do boys. We had a few problems at the Plumleys because they didn't warn us about the boys and they wanted us to be outside and then it rained."

"I hate boys," said Maisie before Sarah had a chance to speak. "There won't be any boys at *my* party. My brother

Matty might come, though, mightn't you, Matty?" She looked towards the door.

'Matty' disappeared before either girl caught sight of him. Sarah was nearly on the floor, but Lianne carried on. "Anyway, Mrs Johnson, you only have to speak to Maisie's friend Megan. She had a great time at Jessica's party, and surely that's a good recommendation."

"Pleeeease, Mum?" whined Maisie.

"What do you charge, again?" asked Mrs Johnson.

"Fifty pounds all in," said Lianne. "And that covers the make-up, trying on the the clothes, our time and travel – everything."

"All right," said Mrs Johnson. "It's what Maisie really wants. The party's on Saturday week at three-thirty."

"Could we just take a peek at where we're going to be?" asked Lianne. "So we know what to expect?"

Sarah shook her head vigorously. She really did not want to bump into Matt. Lianne ignored her.

"I'll show you!" said Maisie, and grabbed Sarah's hand.

"Phew!" said Lianne, when they were back in the street. "I think we're in business again. Smile, Sarah! You can start thinking about what you're going to wear when you go to a party at Matt Johnson's place next week . . ."

"Don't," said Sarah.

"Matty! Bless!" said Lianne, and sniggered.

Uh-oh, thought Sarah.

Ruth

I stayed late at school today. I thought I'd give Choir a try. When I got home, Maisie told me how I'd missed the makeover girls. She said they were nice and one of them, called Sarah, was really pretty. Then I had one of those blinding revelations. Lianne and Sarah are the 'makeover girls'! And they were at my house after school!

So Lianne and Sarah might not like me, but they're coming to my house again on Maisie's birthday and you can bet your bottom dollar that paranoid Matthew will think it's all my fault. That means I'd better stay as far away from them as possible.

Lianne and Sarah both had their reasons for wanting everything to go well at Maisie's party. They went over and over their routine, wrote lists, made a timetable. They were at it constantly, whether a teacher was in front of the class or not.

Ruth had made up with Josie out of guilt. It also made it easier to dissociate herself completely from Lianne and Sarah. And she was able to switch off when Josie was droning on, which meant she could listen in on other conversations, especially ones that contained the word 'makeover'. Sarah and Lianne talked about nothing else.

Lianne was a whirlwind, full of nervous energy. She couldn't wait to do hundreds of makeovers and earn pots of money. She couldn't wait to get Sarah under Matt's nose (not that she talked about it in public) – she relished the idea of matchmaking and was excited at the thought of stage-managing a romance between Sarah and Matt. She didn't quite understand what Sarah saw in him, considering she was gorgeous enough to have anyone. Knowing Sarah, who was soft-hearted or weak-willed, depending on how you looked at it, she probably found his painful shyness attractive! But bringing Sarah and Matt together had become another of Lianne's schemes and, true to form, once she got an idea into her head, she was unstoppable.

Ruth

This is awful. I'm still trying to get my head round the fact that Lianne and Sarah are coming here, to this very house, on Saturday for Maisie's party. They'll find out I live here with Matthew and he'll go ballistic because he'll think his worst fears are coming true. And I'm starting to understand his fears now – I absolutely dread the thought of those two witches knowing about my home life and starting to ask questions about it at school. Well, Lianne's a witch, anyway. (I noticed her fingernails for the first time today. They're about two inches long!) I absolutely have to get away from here before they turn up. That's one problem.

Problem number two concerns Mum. I still don't know whether or not to tell her I'm coming to London, that I'll be a few streets away from her at Emily's. I can't believe I'm even thinking this, but I know that seeing her will be awful and it will make me feel horribly guilty – when really she's the one who should be feeling guilty for sending me here. It would be so much simpler not to tell her I'm coming. There's no reason for her to find out. I can't talk about it properly with Dad. He doesn't really have a clue what it's like for me and Mum, how guilty she makes me feel. I'm kind of assuming he'll pay for my train ticket, since I'm not asking him to drive me. I'm trying to be cool about doing the journey on my own, but even that's a first. So much to sort out. Maybe I will tell Mum. I don't know.

By the Wednesday before the Saturday of Maisie's party Lianne was turbocharged. Sarah was in a complete state about going to Matt Johnson's house, but she decided not to share her terror with Lianne. Lianne would not be sympathetic. Lianne's plan was for Matt to be at his little sister's party, fall instantly in love with Sarah and ask her out then and there. She'd even planned what they should do on their first date (candlelit dinner by the river). To this end she was practising makeovers on Sarah on a daily basis, instructing her what to wear and how to look. Sarah had already decided to wear jeans and a T-shirt, but she played along with Lianne for the sake of a bit of peace.

From ruth@yes.com

Wednesday

Yo Em!

How organised is this? (You can tell I'm desperate.) I'm catching a train at 3.15 which gets in at 4.20, so I hope that gives you enough time to do all your stuff and meet me at Waterloo. I've even ordered a cab to pick me up from here just before 3.00. It's all very convenient because I get away just before Maisie's makeover party begins and the house is overrun with screaming tinies. It's even more important that I get away early because – guess what! – the girls that do the makeovers are none other than Lianne and Sarah from my class, the ones who don't speak to me. Small world, Cobford. I'll fill you in on all that, later.

I'd just got to the point of phoning Mum when she rang me instead. She sounded grisly and said she was feeling so awful, she was glad I wasn't around. She wants to be more "on top of things" so she can enjoy my company. Not exactly what you want to hear from your own mother. Still, it makes things simpler, and if that's the way she wants it . . . So I don't feel too guilty, Em. Just churned up, as usual. It'll be weird, but OK I think.

Must go. See you SOOOOOON!

Rx

*

After all her talk, Lianne arrived at Sarah's house wearing jeans and trainers. She tried to persuade Sarah to dress up, but Sarah managed to stick to her guns. "Remember last time, Lianne. You could hardly tell us from the kids! This is work, and this is my work gear. Anyway, I'm sure Matt won't be there. I've just got this feeling."

"Have it your own way, spoilsport," said Lianne, smiling. "I'm looking forward to this one. I feel I know what to do this time."

"I wish I had your confidence. I'll feel happier once we've started. Is your dad waiting for us in the car?"

"Of course. Best place for him. Have we got everything?"

They drew up outside the Johnsons' house five minutes early, just in time to see a strangely dressed girl, all flapping trousers, grungy coat and scruffy backpack, rushing out of the Johnsons' front door and ducking into a waiting taxi. "Must be some cousin or something, legging it before the mayhem begins," said Lianne. "Weird clothes, though. She should have stayed – she could have done with a makeover!"

At three on the dot a flushed Maisie opened the door and showed them into the living room. "Mum!" she shrieked. "They're here!"

Mrs Johnson appeared but, to Sarah's intense relief, no other members of the family seemed to be around.

"Where's all the rest of your family, Maisie?" asked Lianne bluntly as she and Sarah laid out the clothes on the back of the sofa and created a working area for themselves.

Maisie looked up from stroking a fluffy top. "My brother's gone out," she said. "And Ruth's gone to London."

"Would you like to try something on now, Maisie?" Sarah

asked quickly. "Before your friends arrive. As it's your birth-day?"

"Can I try this fluffy one?" said Maisie.

"Ruth? Who's Ruth?" persisted Lianne.

"I don't know her other name," said Maisie. "Not Johnson, anyway. I really want to try this fluffy one. Now."

Chapter Six

"Spooky to think that a girl about our age was at the Johnsons' house, don't you think?" Lianne was still intrigued by the scruffy figure who had erupted from the Johnsons' house and disappeared into a taxi just as they were arriving.

She and Sarah were working well together now, both reaching into the basket of make-up at the same time. The little girls they were beautifying sat solemnly silent. Those in the queue watched excitedly while the ones who had been done paraded around the room.

Sarah didn't answer.

"Don't you think it's spooky?" Lianne persisted, her fingernails flashing as she dabbed and patted.

"Doesn't the name 'Ruth' ring any bells with you?" Sarah hissed over her little girl's head. "Ruth – who Claire saw talking to Matt Johnson last week?"

Lianne suddenly straightened up. "Oh my God!" she said. "Ruth! Oh my God!" She looked at Sarah in disbelief. "You'd worked it out already, hadn't you? But it didn't *look* like her!"

Sarah's heart sank a little further. "That's because we've only ever seen her in school uniform."

"We'll have to check it out with Mrs Johnson," said

Lianne. "I mean, it can't be a secret if she *lives* here, can it? Maisie didn't talk about Ruth as if she were some special guest." She spent a few minutes plaiting her victim's hair. "Weird, though. Perhaps she's a cousin or something."

"Let's hope so," said Sarah darkly.

"Oh, Sarah – you don't mean – You mean you think she might be Matt's girlfriend or something?" Privately, Lianne doubted that Zit Johnson had a girlfriend.

Sarah looked miserable.

Lianne sprayed some hair colour and paused while it dried. "Anyway, cheer up! We'll soon get to the bottom of it."

The two little girls stood up and admired themselves. "We look wicked!" they chorused. Two more sat down. Sarah had Megan.

"Megan!" said Sarah. "Now, let's make you look beautiful!" And for a while, all thoughts of Ruth were banished.

Ruth

I think Em feels a bit shy too! She sits in the front of the car and I sit in the back. Her mum, Sue, is great – she seems almost as pleased to see me as Em. "Ruth – how lovely to see you again! Emily's missed you so much! Your feet won't touch the ground while you're here. Em's got so much planned, haven't you, Em?"

She has. Shopping with what's left of the afternoon. Meeting up with a bunch of kids from school downstairs in Starbucks. Home for a video and a curry and then she's got a few more plans, but she's not discussing them in front of her mother.

Excellent. I feel happier than I've felt for at least three

weeks. Now Em's gossiping away. I can't get enough of it. There's so much to catch up on.

"How's your mum, Ruth?" Sue's voice cuts through the conversation. I realise we're driving past our house. It's so weird. "Emily says you're not planning to visit her?"

"She doesn't want to see me."

"That can't be true, surely!"

"More to the point, she doesn't want *me* to see *her*. She's lost even more weight, apparently."

"Oh dear. Maybe I should call in on her one day."

"I'll see her next time. I – I never told her I was coming."

"That's up to you, love. I think a good time is probably what you need right now."

It's as if my Cobford life never happened. Emily and I have cruised round the charity shops as per usual, been into Smiths and Boots and Virgin, the jewellery shops and the two shops that sell cards and candles and gorgeous things. We cram on to the sofas in Starbucks with all my old friends. Most of us have been together since primary school. We all dress pretty much the same way. I just feel so comfortable! It's great. Two of the boys, Charlie and Luke, seem to have grown taller overnight. Em fancies Charlie, I can tell. I can almost imagine myself fancying Luke, but I'm not sure what I feel about boys right now. There's been too much else going on, I guess.

"Honestly, Lianne, you could have been a bit more tactful."

"Well, we need to know, don't we?"

"Maybe, but when she said, 'Ruth's just living with us for a while,' you should have realised that she didn't want to say any more."

"You're so ungrateful. I was only asking for your sake."

"You girls all right in the back there?" asked Lianne's dad.

"Fine, Dad." Lianne wanted to justify herself. "Anyway, Sarah, I only asked if Ruth was a relation."

"And she ignored you."

"Whatever. We're still fifty quid richer! This is Sarah's road, Dad. You can drop her here."

Lianne didn't get out of the car with Sarah. Sarah knew that Lianne wasn't happy with her. "Bye!" she called wanly. She lugged her case round to the kitchen door and let herself in.

"Tired out, are you, sweetheart?" asked her mum.

"Totally!" said Sarah, and relaxed into the warmth of her family.

Ruth

Emily's Saturday-night plan was just like all the other plans for Saturday nights we'd ever had. It started big – about twenty of us were going to meet up in the park at half past nine and then go round to someone's house where the parents were away and an older brother was in charge. We spent ages getting dressed up. Emily and I like the same sort of clothes, so it didn't matter that I hadn't brought much with me – I could borrow anything of hers. Her mobile never stopped ringing. In the end, five of us were going to meet in the park. Then two more people rang back to say they were bailing on us. So Hannah, the only one left, who lives round the corner, came over. Like us, she was all dressed up with nowhere to go. We went into the back garden and shivered while Hannah tried to smoke two cigarettes one after the other and then we went in and watched another video.

Emily was really apologetic, but I didn't mind at all. "It's just like old times, Em," I said. "The day we get our act together and actually go out once we've got dressed up, things will all start to change."

"I kind of hoped Charlie would be in the park tonight, though," said Emily.

"We're all waiting with bated breath for something to happen there," said Hannah to me, and I had a quick twinge of feeling left out, of things moving on without me. Anyway, Emily had me this weekend, didn't she? Why should she want Charlie?

"I didn't realise you were that keen, Em," I said.

"Well – you know..." Em gave me a hug. "Anyway, you're here. I don't need Charlie. He probably doesn't fancy me anyway."

Early on Sunday morning Sarah reached over to her bedside table to answer her mobile. It was Lianne's number.

"Hi, Sarah. It's me. I've been thinking about Ruth and I've had an idea. Can I come over?"

"No one's really up yet, Lianne." Sarah was never very good at putting Lianne off, even when she wanted to, like now. She realised that Lianne was trying to make it up, but she still felt wounded after yesterday. And Ruth was the last person she wanted to think about. Could it possibly be that Ruth and Matt were an *item*?

"You could come over this evening, I suppose. I'll try and get my homework done a bit earlier."

"Cool. Can I come for supper?"

"I s'pose so."

Ruth

On Sunday morning, Emily and I sat in bed and just talked and talked. It was so much better than being on the phone or emailing. Em thought Matthew was being totally pathetic, not wanting people to know I lived with him. "Foxy lady like you – you'd think he'd be proud."

"Huh. Mind you, you haven't met him. I kind of know where he's coming from about wanting to keep home and school separate, but he's got problems I don't understand. Sometimes I think I don't understand anyone at King Edward's."

"So you keep saying. What d'you mean, exactly?"

"If you saw them, you'd know. They're just different. It's hard to explain. These girls, Lianne and Sarah, they're sort of –"

"Go on. I'm sure it'll do you good to put it in words. I know that's what my mum would say. They're obviously bugging you."

"Well, the truth is – I suppose I want them to like me. But they obviously don't. And I don't know why they don't. I suppose I'm just too – too … Oh, I don't know."

"OK. Let me try. You're probably too grungey and laid-back for them. Deep down, they know you're dead trendy, but they're still at the sparkly stage. You know, the one that comes after the pink stage. It comes from wearing uniform all week, I'm sure. We've always looked down on sparkly people, you and me."

"Precisely. Perhaps it shows. Perhaps they think I'm stuck up?"

"It's always a possibility."

"I am, you know. I do feel superior somehow. I'm snooty about Josie too, but she's so desperate, she doesn't care. But there's no way Lianne and Sarah are going to let me act superior around them. Especially Lianne. I just can't stand being a nobody, Em. People like us aren't used to being nobodies, are we?"

"Perhaps when you go back you should be a bit more interested in them. I mean, why don't you just tell them you're

Maisie's stepsister, or whatever, and that – oh my goodness – they were at your house, etc. etc? Make friends?"

"Matthew would kill me!"

"Well, forget Matthew. What's he ever done for you? Just suck up to them a bit."

"I'm not like that."

"I'm bored with your Lianne and Sarah. Let's go down and microwave the rest of the curry for breakfast and watch telly. Then Mum said she'd drive us to Camden Market. Got to make the most of every minute!"

"Let's talk about Ruth Miller, then."

"She's not so bad. Though if she's going out with Matt, I hate her."

"I'm sure she's not going out with Matt. I'm sure there's an obvious answer."

"Which we'll never find out."

"But we will. That's my idea. Let's just be friendly and –"

"You're never *just* friendly, Lianne. Except to me, of course. Everyone knows that."

"Well thanks a lot."

"Most people are a bit scared of you." Sarah said this with feeling.

"Good. Anyway. Let's just go up to her and say we saw her leaving Matt's house at the weekend. How does she know the Johnsons? We'll say it in a friendly sort of way. Maybe we should go all wide-eyed and ask for an introduction to Matt because we think he's cute. That would soon sort it out!"

"And you don't think that will scare her off?"

"OK. Let's just sit with her at lunch, in a friendly sort of way, and then ask her. Oh, come on, Sarah! I'm only doing this for you, you know!"

"That's what you said before, and I'm not sure I believe it. But all right. I don't mind making friends. I think she might be quite nice."

"Just so long as you remember I'm your best friend, Sarah. Lianne and Sarah rule! OK?"

"OK."

Ruth

It was almost harder leaving Emily's than it was leaving home three weeks ago. I had such a brilliant time. A totally, wonderfully, brilliant time. I wish we could afford for me to go back to London every weekend. I feel funny about not seeing Mum though. I'll ring her tonight. I won't say anything about being in London, but I want to know how she is.

I suppose Lianne and Sarah will be going on about Maisie's makeover party to their friends tomorrow. They might talk about Angela and Matthew (though I know he made himself scarce for the party, too). And the house. What if they're rude about it all?

I miss Emily and everyone so much already.

Chapter Seven

"Can we sit here?"

Ruth looked up. "Oh? Oh, yes, fine." She moved down a seat so Lianne and Sarah could sit next to her at the table in the canteen.

"Good chips!" said Lianne.

"Yep." Ruth wondered fearfully what was coming next.

"And then . . . " said Josie, on Ruth's left, annoyed at being interrupted, "when we switched on the underwater lights, only two of them worked!"

"I think you're mistaking us for people who might be interested in swimming pools, Josie," said Lianne smoothly, "but you'd be wrong. Wouldn't she, Ruth?"

Ruth didn't know what to say. The joy of not having to spend an entire lunch hour with Josie was in danger of making her unkind. "Well – I have heard quite a bit about it already."

"Exactly," said Lianne. "Now, run along, Josie, and find someone your own size to play with."

Ruth and Sarah both saw Josie flush, before scraping back her chair and stumbling away, hurt, but neither quite had the courage to chide Lianne about it until it was too late.

"Lianne!" said Sarah severely, but smiling nonetheless.

That was so typical of Lianne – to be cruel to someone in a way that made it hard not to laugh.

"Well!" said Lianne, admiring her nails. "Honestly. What a tub of lard!"

Far too late, Ruth tried. "She is my friend, you know. Sort of."

"I think you can do better than that," said Lianne. "Anyway. We wanted to talk to you because it seems you already have friends in high places."

"High places?" said Ruth.

"Yeah. I'm sure you've heard about our fantastic kids' makeover business? Well, we were doing one at a little girl's house on Saturday – Maisie Johnson? Matt Johnson's little sister?"

"We thought we saw you leaving their house, and . . . " Sarah began, but then halted. She didn't want to let on what she felt about Matt.

Lianne broke in. "I thought you said you didn't know Matt Johnson?"

Ruth wasn't going to be intimidated. She couldn't tell what connections they'd made or how much she could give away. She didn't altogether rate these two, but she longed to be part of what was going on, not to be treated as a nobody. "Well, I don't really *know* him," she said, as evenly as she could. "For a start, I don't think of Matthew as 'Matt'. The Johnsons are sort of – family friends. Our parents know each other." That was true enough.

It was a good answer. It silenced both Sarah and Lianne. Lianne was just considering challenging Ruth with the fact that Mrs Johnson had said she lived there when suddenly Ruth looked around anxiously and abruptly stood up. "Got to go!" she said.

Ruth

Lianne and Sarah are definitely on to me. I spotted Matthew outside the canteen window and got away from them as quickly as I could. I know Em thinks I should forget him, but worrying about him has become a habit. He didn't appear for breakfast this morning and I know it was because he's angry about Lianne and Sarah coming to our house. Probably the same old thing – he doesn't want people at school knowing about his home life. I don't want to make it worse right now.

"What got into her?" Lianne was affronted.

"Probably doesn't like people asking questions," said Sarah.

"Aha. Then something interesting must be going on. She's not telling the whole truth. Why didn't she admit she was living with them? But she can't stay away from us for long. We'll just have to catch up with her in class."

"Let's not pressure her," said Sarah. "She can tell us in her own time. Why don't I ask her back to my house?"

"Not without me, you don't," said Lianne.

"As if I would. This Thursday, then?"

"OK."

Mr Booth tipped back in his chair and observed his form as they banged and clattered their way in to afternoon registration. It was how he learned about them – who was on top, who was being left out. The near-inseparable Lianne and Sarah came in almost last. He saw Lianne nudge Sarah and Sarah walk over to Ruth's desk to deliver a folded-up note. He watched Ruth's expression as she read the note – part anxious, part pleased. "Quiet!" he yelled, and stood up to make himself heard above the din.

Ruth

*Sarah has asked me over to her place after school on
Thursday. With Lianne, of course. I'm sort of flattered. I
think I want to go, but how long before I have to come clean
about living with Matthew? It's crazy pretending I don't
know him if they actually saw me leaving the house. It's just
that I have this sneaking feeling that taking me on as well
as my dad made something worse for him and, believe me,
I can get behind those feelings. Maybe I should talk to
Dad or Angela about it. I still don't want to dump him in it,
though. Not speaking to Matt in school didn't seem
quite such an unreasonable request at first. Maybe it still
isn't. Dunno any more. Anyway, at least I did the decent
thing today and apologised to Josie. I feel sorry for
her, too.*

"Are you coming on Thursday, then?" Lianne was on Ruth's
case straight after school.

"It's to Sarah's, isn't it?"

"Yes, but I live there half the time, don't I, Sarah?"

"Always on a Thursday, anyway," said Sarah. "Can you
come, Ruth? Can you cope with big families?"

"Yeah, sure."

"You can walk back with us on Thursday then – unless
you'll want to go home and change first."

"Nah," said Ruth, "I'll go with you."

"Do you want to walk home with us now?" Lianne was
being over-friendly and Sarah could see Ruth recoiling
slightly.

"It's OK, thanks. I'm busy tonight. See you tomorrow!"
Ruth headed off in the opposite direction. She needed more

time to get used to the idea of Lianne and Sarah being her mates.

Ruth

From ruth@yes.com
Monday night.
Hiya Em, how's it goin'?

Guess what – I've got the big invitation . . . After everything I told you at the weekend, Lianne and Sarah have suddenly got all friendly. I dread to think why, precisely. They've got it out of me that I vaguely know Matthew, but I'm not volunteering any more information unless they ask direct questions. The things I do for Matthew!

More later.

Rxxx

I've just rung Mum. She sounded so bad. Little tiny voice and lots of coughing. Kept saying how much she'd love to see my face and how much she misses me. It makes me feel even worse about not telling her I was five minutes away at the weekend. Thing is, I miss her too. I feel cross with her for being like this. Sometimes I feel cross with her for driving Dad away. I mean, when Mum's like this, I'd prefer Angela. Except that Mum's my mum and . . .

Best not to go too deep on that one . . . I can hear Matthew stomping around downstairs. I think I shall curl up in a very small ball on my bed. It makes me feel little and safe and about six years old.

"Granny, this is Ruth. She's just started in our class. She wanted to come and see your annexe."

"Fine old world where the aged are annexed from the rest of life, isn't it?" said Sarah's grandmother, holding out her hand to Ruth.

"That's not fair, Granny!" said Sarah. "You'd hate being in with us noisy lot. You're always saying so."

It was a beautiful autumn afternoon and Granny's corner of the garden caught the late sunshine. Millie lay stretched out beside her chair and Ruth crouched down to pet the little dog. Lianne was still indoors, on her mobile, trying to fix up the next Makeover date after the success of Maisie Johnson's. Ruth could just catch her businesslike voice as she tried to sell their services.

Ruth looked around at Sarah's home, so unlike anywhere in London. It was a pretty house, rambling and quite scruffy, with Granny's annexe almost the size of another small house, and all sorts of ramshackle sheds and outbuildings further down the garden. There were neighbouring houses in sight, but only just.

Sarah ran up the garden in answer to a yell from Lianne. "Back in a sec," she said, and left Ruth and Granny alone together.

"What are you making?" Ruth asked politely, picking up Granny's sewing that lay on the grass.

"Oh, just a little dress for Bronwen. I always like to have something on the go."

"It's beautiful. I love beautifully made clothes. That's why I like buying old clothes from charity shops. No one seems to make things by hand any more."

"You're right, pet, we're a dying breed! Mind you, Sarah's interested to learn. I've helped her knock up some little outfits before now. I don't suppose they teach you dress-making at school any more, do they?"

Just then, Lianne and Sarah came out of the house shriek-ing and punching the air. "We're gonna be LOADED!" shouted Lianne. "TWO more gigs!"

"In three weeks' time," cautioned Sarah. "And then another in five weeks."

"Well, that's OK," said Lianne. And then, "Oh no, Sarah. We can't do that second one!"

"Why not?" asked Ruth, caught up in the excitement.

"Because it's the week just after half term – when we go on the geography field trip." Lianne pulled out her mobile and stabbed out the number again. "I'll ring them back. See if we can do it either the weekend before or the weekend after." Lianne walked back towards the house.

"She doesn't waste any time, does she?" said Granny. "I haven't heard about a field trip, Sarah. Does your mother know about it?"

"She'll have had all the letters. Can't say I knew when it was. Lianne probably remembered because she likes going away from home. She doesn't do it much."

"She spends half her time here. That's away from home."

"Did you know about it, Ruth?"

"Vaguely." Matthew had been the year before and men-tioned it when Ruth brought the letter home. "I'm still getting used to being in Cobford, so I haven't thought too much about going even further away from London. Is it good?"

"It's just one of those things you do in Year Nine. About the only thing you *do* do in Year Nine. There's this place in Wales where our school always goes. And we have discos and things – as well as getting wet."

"Is it compulsory?" asked Ruth nervously. She wasn't sure she fancied being twice-removed from home.

"Everyone always goes, if that's what you mean. They put up the photos in the exhibition area by the canteen afterwards. It looks cool."

Lianne rejoined them, snapping her phone shut triumphantly. "Didn't I do well? We're going to do our first mid-week makeover. On young Tamsin's eighth birthday. Megan and Maisie have *so* been putting the word about! We're famous!" Lianne put one arm round Sarah and the other, less comfortably, round Ruth. "Come on, guys, let's go and steal some ice cream from Sarah's freezer. It's ages until we'll get a proper meal round here."

"Don't mind me," said Granny, good-natured still, but a little put out at Lianne depriving her of her companions. "We'll talk again another time," she said to Ruth as the other two girls dragged her away.

They dug a tub of Ben & Jerry's from the freezer and took it up to Sarah's room. "What happens at these makeover parties, then?" asked Ruth.

Thirty minutes later, she wished she hadn't. The two of them were still yakking on and on. Ruth inadvertently glanced at her watch.

"We boring you?" asked Lianne, quick as a flash.

"No, no!" said Ruth. "It's really cool. But I don't know how you cope with little kids. I can't stand them – not in big numbers anyway."

"Wait till you meet my family," said Sarah. "Kids are OK. I'm used to them. They don't scare me."

"Maisie Johnson and her friends must have liked us," said Lianne. "Or they wouldn't all be asking for makeover parties."

"Where did you get the clothes?" asked Ruth, changing the subject a little. She thought the clothes were totally naff, but she could see how they might appeal to little girls.

"Cute, aren't they?" said Lianne proudly. "My mum runs a children's clothes shop – Little Tigers, you might have seen it – we got them from her. Then if the kids want to buy the clothes for themselves, they can get a discount in her shop. So everyone does well out of it."

There was a commotion downstairs as Sarah's mother arrived home with the younger ones. "How many little brothers and sisters have you got?" asked Ruth.

"Just Freddie and Bronwen. There's only eleven months between my brother Ben and me. Mum said we were such hard work it took her five years to get round to wanting more children."

Bronnie burst in on cue. Ruth thought she looked a lot like Sarah.

"Hi, Bronnie. Shall we all come downstairs now? Is there something good on TV?"

Bronwen went silent with shyness and stuck her thumb in her mouth, so Sarah picked her up and all four girls went down into the living room.

Sarah's mother put her head round the door. "Hello. It's Ruth, isn't it? I've heard all about you. Tea in – " She saw that they'd just embarked on their favourite soap. "Tea in half an hour, girls. Is macaroni cheese all right for you, Ruth – " Ruth thanked her and settled back comfortably into the sofa.

Sarah's dad came home with Ben after the girls had eaten. Like Bronwen, Ben was shy. "Hey, Ben," said Sarah, "say hello to Ruth! Ruth, this is my brother Ben."

"Hi, Ruth," said Ben and quickly went upstairs, but not before Ruth had felt a stab of jealousy at such a natural exchange.

"Do you want a lift home, Ruth?" asked Sarah's mum. "before Sarah's dad takes his coat off?"

"No, no, thank you," said Ruth. "Unless you want to get rid of me? My dad's picking me up in a quarter of an hour." Ruth was glad she had arranged that one. She didn't want any more probing questions about Matt Johnson.

Ruth

I finally had a showdown with Matthew. It went like this:

"Why does it have to be a secret that I live with you, Matthew? I don't want secrets, OK? I've just made friends with these two girls and I've had to spend the whole time changing the subject and being careful what I say. And I'm not going to do it any more."

"What two girls?"

"You know, Lianne and Sarah. The ones that did Maisie's party."

"I thought as much. Which is exactly why I don't want you telling people. I know what girls are like. They'll ask you questions about whether I shave or not and what colour boxer shorts I wear and do I wear pyjamas ... And then they'll kill themselves laughing about my – complexion."

"Why on earth should they do that?"

"Everyone else does. How would you like your nickname to be Zit, eh? And those two fell about giggling when they gave me their stupid flyer. Wish I'd thrown it back in their faces now, then this would never have happened."

"You're so wrong, Matthew. They don't give a toss about you. I've tried to be understanding and do what you want so far, but this is about me now. I just want to be able to tell people where I live and who I live with. I won't make a big thing of it. I just can't lie – and I really don't see why I should. So you can stop being so selfish for once!"

I flounced out. I'd had enough. I didn't care what Matthew thought any more.

From ruth@yes.com
Thursday night
Dear Em

Wish you were here to talk to. If I had a mobile I'd ring you, but I don't want to come out of my room – hence the email. Good thing: I've just been over to Sarah's house and had a nice time. Bad thing: I've just had a barney with Matthew – told him I'm not going to pretend I don't know him any more.

From Emily356@yes.net
Hi Roo! Good on yer! You tell him!

I'm still up, as you've probably gathered. Stay on line and we can chat – until Dad wants the computer.

So, why do you think L and S want to be friends all of a sudden?

From ruth@yes.com
Apart from the fact that I am a wonderful and fascinating individual? Dunno. It seems to have something to do with Matthew.

From Emily356@yes.net
Perhaps they fancy him.

From ruth@yes.com
I doubt it! He's got this really terrible skin, you see. I don't

notice after all this time, tho actually, it is clearing up a bit, and I suppose some people might find him good looking underneath. He's quite tall. Got dark hair, in a weird hairstyle.

From Emily356@yes.net
ROO! What are you telling me here?

From ruth@yes.com
Don't be daft! I do not fancy him. Anyway, he's my stepbrother.

From Emily356@yes.net
Perhaps they fancy him and they think you're his girlfriend?

From ruth@yes.com
Duh! Just because you like Charlie, don't try to invent a boyfriend for me!

Miss you loads, Em. I shouldn't have to be struggling with making new friends at my age! Still, here I am trailing round after Lianne and Sarah. I always thought of them as two of a kind, but now I can see they're quite different. Sarah is OK in a sweet and innocent sort of way. She seems to have a very cosy life. Lianne is dead sharp, but dangerous, if you know what I mean. Maybe you'd better come and visit me – see all these weirdos in the flesh.

Just as I was pressing send, there was a tap on my door. It was Matthew. "Sorry I lost my rag back there," he said.

I knew it cost him a lot to apologise.

"Me too," I said.

I looked at him. He'd had a shower and his hair was wet and tousled, not stupid. I noticed too that his skin was smoother than I'd seen it for a long time. I didn't fancy him – no way! But I felt, well, sisterly.

"I promise I won't ever discuss you with them, Matthew. I'll swear to it."

"Really?"

"Really." We didn't hug, Matthew and me. Not even in a brotherly/sisterly sort of way, it just wouldn't feel right, but I wanted to do something to show him that I cared, that I understood. "Matthew?"

"What?"

"They'll have to give you another nickname."

"Why's that?"

"You can't call someone Zit if they haven't really got spots any more, can you?"

Matthew's smile lit up the room.

"You're not wrong, Ruth," he said. "'Night!" And he positively bounced out.

I checked for a reply from Em before I switched off.

Emily356@yes.net
I might just do that! Watch this space.
Nightie night.
Em xx

"Hey, guys . . . " Ruth sat down beside Lianne and Sarah next day at lunch. "I've got a confession to make. I'm sorry I was less than honest with you, but I had my reasons. I live with Matt Johnson. I'm sort of his common-law stepsister."

"We already knew you lived there," said Lianne, coolly. "His mother told us."

"But we didn't know you were related," said Sarah, smiling hugely.

"Here's the deal," Ruth said, before they got too carried away. "You know I live with him now, but he's absolutely not up for discussion under any circumstances. OK? He's kind of a private sort of guy."

Lianne rolled her eyes at Sarah, but gave Ruth a mock-salute. "You're the boss," she said.

Ruth took that as agreement, though she knew already that the question of who was boss in this situation was never going to be that simple.

Chapter Eight

Lianne appraised Ruth coolly as she walked into school the next morning, as if giving her marks out of ten. Ticking mental boxes that all said INCORRECT, she took in the velvet shoulder bag, the straggly hair, the knee-length skirt, the heavy shoes on the ends of legs in black tights. And that was just for starters . . .

Lianne dug her elbow into Sarah's ribs. "We'll have to take Ruth in hand if she's going to hang around with us," she said.

"Is she going to?" asked Sarah. "Hang around with us?"

"Well, you must want her to," said Lianne, "now we've got to know her. Think how much easier it will be to get to know Matt Johnson if you're mates with his stepsister!"

"But you know we can't talk about him, Lianne!"

"We'll talk about whatever we want. She doesn't know you like him. Yet."

Sarah felt vulnerable all of a sudden.

Ruth Miller raised a hand in greeting to Josie, but headed for Lianne and Sarah. The three of them walked into the classroom together.

Ruth

I appear to have friends. Once you're in with Lianne and Sarah, you're in with everybody. Lianne really seems to want to be my mate, but I don't want to split her and Sarah up. I don't even want to be her mate. I can't say I really like her. Compared with Emily … But no one's ever going to match up to Emily.

I've checked my email and she hasn't sent anything today. I expect she will over the weekend.

From ruth@yes.com
Hi Em

It's Saturday night. Nowhere to go, as usual. Matthew's not around. Maisie's at a sleepover. Dad and Angela are watching a DVD.

Need to chat, Em. It's got better at school with these new friends, but I still need to talk to you.

No reply.

From ruth@yes.com
Hi Em

Sunday night. Where are you? Angela's been on the phone practically all day, so if you rang and didn't leave a message I won't be able to tell. It's quite late and I don't feel like coming out of my room – it's too cosy in here.

School again tomorrow and I'm not dreading it as much as usual because at least someone will talk to me. And at least Matthew and I have cleared the air a bit. Matthew seemed to believe me when I said I wouldn't talk about him. (It's not as if I want to, and I can't think why anyone else would be interested either. I just don't buy your theory that Sarah and

Lianne fancy him. I mean, we're talking Matthew here! I think
he's just a friend 'in high places' because he's in the year
above us. And a boy.)

Please reply!!!

Still no reply.

Lianne, as usual, didn't waste any time. "Hope you don't
mind my saying this . . . " she said to Ruth at break on
Monday.

Sarah hung back a little.

Ruth braced herself. "It's just that, if you'd let me help
you, you could look so much *better* in your uniform. I mean,
it's not as if you're unattractive or anything. But we're used
to uniform, aren't we, Sarah? And we know what to do to
make it look, sort of *trendy*."

"What, right now?" asked Ruth.

Lianne's long nails were at Ruth's throat undoing her tie.
"Let me show you."

"Don't throttle her," squeaked Sarah, alarmed.

Ruth stood, chin up, with her back to the wall as Lianne
retied her tie so the knot was fat and the ends were short.
"There!" said Lianne, folding Ruth's collar down into a
sharp crease and patting the tie. "That makes you look more
normal."

Ruth ignored the 'normal' dig , but said instead, "I don't
know how you made it look, Lianne. I couldn't see how you
were tying it from upside down."

"We'll show you," said Sarah, kindly.

"There's all sorts of other things you could do," said
Lianne. The buzzer was going for the start of the next lesson.
"Get rid of that bag for a start."

"But I like my bag," said Ruth, wounded.

"No you don't," said Lianne. "A sports bag is what you want. You can have my old one if you want."

Ruth didn't know what to say.

"It's hardly *old*," said Sarah, thinking it was the idea of Lianne's cast-offs rather than sports bags in general that rendered Ruth speechless. "She bought the old one when I bought this one."

They filed into the classroom. "We'll sort you out on Thursday," said Lianne. "Don't worry."

Ruth

From ruth@yes.com
Hi Em

It's Monday night and I've just had a completely different day at school from all the other ones this term. Lianne and Sarah want to make me over so I look like them. I'm not going to tell you how because you'd only laugh. It's nice having people to talk to, but I'd rather be with you any day.

Please reply.

I really want to hear back from Em. I tried ringing her after school and left a message, but she hasn't called me back. What's so important that she can't ring me? And she's not replying to my emails. I need her to keep me grounded because I'm in danger of losing touch with my real self with all this attention from Lianne and Sarah. I'm only friends with them because there's no one else. And because I'm every bit as cool as they are, if not cooler.

Matthew commented on my tie this evening. "Tie looks better," he said.

"So why did you let me go on wearing it the other way for so long?" I asked.

"Assumed you liked it that way," he said, turning back to the TV.

As if I liked it any way. Disgusting green stripy thing. I don't really want to have a uniform makeover. I hate it so much I'd rather just wear it in all its nastiness to show my contempt.

I quite like looking individual.

I think.

"Do you want to come to my place on Thursday?" Sarah asked Ruth. "Lianne and I can help you with your uniform. She's going to bring her old sports bag for you."

"I've already asked her to come to mine on Thursday," said Lianne. "Haven't I, Ruth?"

"Sort of," said Ruth, embarrassed.

"Oh," said Sarah, not sure what to make of this turn of events. Was she invited to Lianne's on Thursday? She sometimes felt fed up with Lianne for taking Thursdays at her house for granted, but this was a bit sudden.

"You're coming too," said Lianne. "Thought it would make a change. There's loads of amazing meals in our freezer and we'll have the house to ourselves."

"Oh," said Sarah. "OK."

Ruth

I finally got an email from Emily on Wednesday. She didn't answer any of my questions. She didn't say why she hadn't replied at the weekend. She just went on about how cute Charlie is and what Hannah thinks she ought to do about him.

So much for reminding me of who I am. I think she's forgotten I'm her best friend.

Perhaps I'm not now. Perhaps I'm now this uniform person.

I've tried doing the tie myself, but I can't get it right. Angela doesn't know how to do it, and I don't feel I can involve Matthew. He really isn't any use, that boy. I can't believe how worried by it I am. It's only a tie! I'm going over to Liannne's after school tonight and she and Sarah are going to tell me all I need to know to become Cobford woman.

Emily won't recognise me.

Lianne was queening it. She linked her arm in Ruth's and went on about her wonderful house and high-powered parents all the way home. When the pavement wasn't wide enough Sarah had to hop up and down the kerb or walk behind. She'd heard it all before. It was weird hearing Lianne talking up a home life that she knew was empty.

Lianne's house smelled of air freshener and closed windows. All the kitchen surfaces were immaculate. Lianne went to the fridge. "Coke, anyone?" She handed round the ice-cold cans. "Let's go up to my room. I've dug out the bag for you, Ruth. Mum was about to chuck it out."

Lianne's bedroom was immaculate, too. "The cleaner's moved everything!" grumbled Lianne. "I left the bag on the bed. I bet she's put it underneath."

While Lianne looked under her bed, Sarah offered to show Ruth how to tie the tie. "You can practise on me," she said. "I'll take you through it step by step."

Lianne drew back from under the bed with the sports bag. "Here you are, Ruth! Now you can chuck out that old thing. Can I do your hair now?" She grabbed a hank and twisted it back. "You see? It really suits you pulled back off your face. You can see your cheekbones!"

Ruth decided to succumb. If this was friendship, then she'd take it. Lianne tied her hair back tightly. She showed her exactly how much to roll her skirt over at the waistband to get the perfect length. "Short is good," Sarah said. Lianne produced a pair of socks and made Ruth exchange them for her tights. The socks were identical to the ones Sarah and Lianne wore. "We can't do anything about your shoes, though," said Sarah. "You've got big feet. You'll have to buy new ones."

The three of them went into Lianne's parents' bedroom and stood in front of the big mirror. "See?" said Lianne. "Now you look like us."

Ruth could hardly tell which one was her.

Tea was not good, because the freezer contained mostly fish and several exotic Chinese dinners. No pizza. They found some oven chips and cooked them, but they took a long time. Lianne fried some eggs, but they broke and the yolks were hard and dry. There was plenty of ice cream, which they ate in front of the telly until Sarah's dad came to pick her up.

"It's not even late!" complained Lianne. "You'll stay a bit longer, won't you, Ruth?"

"My dad's on his way, too, I'm afraid," said Ruth, realising that they'd be leaving Lianne on her own.

"Will you be OK, Lianne?" asked Sarah. She knew how much Lianne hated waiting alone in the house for her mum to get back.

"I can look after myself," said Lianne sharply. "Anyway, Sarah, just because you have me over on Thursdays, don't think you're doing me such a big favour – allowing me to be surrounded by your precious, cosy family."

Sarah was used to this sort of outburst, but Ruth was shocked. "Wasn't that a bit harsh, Lianne?" she ventured, when Sarah had left.

"Nah," said Lianne. "Sometimes I think I'm growing out of Sarah. She can be a bit childish. Not like us." She reached for a nail file. "Come on. I can give you a manicure while we wait for your dad."

Ruth proffered her uneven nails and hoped her dad wouldn't be long.

From ruth@yes.com
Hi Em

It's me again. HELP! I'm turning into a green person! What can I do? I'm stuck here with green people, so maybe it's best if I turn into one. What else can I do?

It took her ages to reply. Em's no use these days. Every time I talk to her or email her about how difficult it is being a green person, back she comes with some little snippet about Charlie – how Charlie looked at her, or how Charlie had had a haircut, or how funny Charlie was at lunch time. And if it's not Charlie, it's Hannah. Sometimes I wonder if she ever thinks about me at all.

Over the next couple of weeks, Mr Booth observed that Lianne and Sarah had taken on Ruth Miller in a big way. He wasn't sure how much she was enjoying the friendship, but it was good to see that she was no longer an outsider. What's more, Ruth had started to look a little different. She had a new sports bag instead of her old velvet one and she didn't hide behind her hair as much as she had done at first. She tied her tie with a fat knot like the other trendy girls did and started to wear her socks at precisely the fashionable height. She seemed to spend more time with Lianne, which surprised him. He imagined she'd have got on better with Sarah.

Ruth

The days are grinding by. I've been here an unbelievable five weeks. Five weeks without seeing Mum. Five weeks without Em. So I've taken Lianne on recently. It distracts me from Matthew's moods, Mum's phone calls and Em's lack of emails. Lianne thinks it's the other way round, I'm sure. She thinks she's taken me on. She seriously gives me helpful hints on 'being popular'! I've gone along with it, but I can't begin to tell Emily about this – she'd laugh herself sick. As I would, if it was happening to someone else. The thing is, I feel like someone else. I feel like the person I've made up for Lianne. The green disguise is like armour. It protects the poor little grub inside.

"What's up, Sarah?" Granny wasn't used to seeing her granddaughter like this. She watched her burying her face in Millie's fur and stroking the little dogs' ears.

"Nothing."

"Oh, come on. You can tell your old granny. I won't pass it on. Is it your friends?"

"Sort of."

"Something to do with the new girl? I liked her. I thought you and she would get on."

"She seems to be Lianne's friend, now."

"Really? I thought she was more like you. Nice-natured."

"Lianne's nice." Sarah defended Lianne out of habit.

"Of course she is, pet."

"It's just that I feel like a spare part, some days. Even when they come here. They're coming tomorrow."

"Lianne always comes on a Thursday, doesn't she?"

"Nearly always, yes. But now she invites Ruth along as well, without even asking me first," Sarah almost snarled. "And we never get to visit Ruth at the Johnsons' house. It's not fair."

Part of Sarah's problem was that their friendship with Ruth seemed to put Matt even further out of reach. She knew Ruth wasn't a rival, but she was amazingly adept at sidestepping questions about her stepbrother and Lianne seemed to have given up asking them. The pair of them had a way of making Sarah feel less mature than they were.

It was the Thursday before the next makeover party. Lianne and Sarah realised that they were out of practice. "Can we do you, Ruth?" asked Lianne. "Please, pretty please?"

"What, and make me look like an eight-year-old?" laughed Ruth. "I don't generally do make-up, but I suppose so. Leave my clothes alone, though. I adore my divine green uniform."

Sarah looked surprised.

"Joke, Sarah," said Ruth.

"Oh, Sarah," said Lianne. "You didn't really think she meant it, did you?"

"Course not," said Sarah hotly. "We'd better check the clothes, though. Did we wash them last time? I can't remember."

"You check the clothes," said Lianne. "I'll put make-up on Ruth. Now, sit still, Ruth. Take off your glasses."

Great, thought Sarah. She opened the case of clothes and

tipped them on to her bed. Next thing she'll be asking Ruth to do the makeovers with us and split the money three ways.

"Maybe you should join our Makeover business, Ruth?" said Lianne.

"Cheers, but –" Ruth had to close her mouth as Lianne wielded the lipstick.

"Sarah won't mind, will you, Sarah?" asked Lianne.

Sarah didn't know what to say.

"No, honestly," said Ruth, her eyes shut as Lianne stroked mascara on to her eyelashes. "It's not my thing. And I'm often not around at weekends. Have to go home and see my mum. You know."

Ruth

I might pass myself off as one of them at school, but they can't honestly think I want to join their makeover business. As if. Anyway, I don't think Sarah likes the idea much. Then again, I suppose I could go along this weekend. It's not as if I've got anything else to do.

I'll just check my email. I'm due one from Em. Not that it will say anything non-Charlie-related.

Emily356@yes.net
Roo, baby!

Guess what? Charlie's asked me out!!!! This Saturday!!!! The day after tomorrow! Hannah kept saying she thought he was about to make a move. He was so cute and shy about it. Started talking in long words: "Would you like to accompany me . . . " Oooh, Roo, I am soooo HAPPY!!!! I don't know what to wear. We're only going to see a film – the six o'clock performance and then have a pizza afterwards. I can't think of anything else right now. Watch this space!!!

Love from your happy happy happy Emxxxx

Great. So glad she's missing me.

Dad came in looking worried. "Ruth, your mum's just been on the phone."

"Oh. I didn't hear it. Has she rung off?"

"I think I ought to take you to see her this weekend."

"What? Why? Has something happened?"

Dad scratched his head. "Nothing specific. She just didn't sound too good."

Huh, I thought. She's finally got to you.

"Let's go on Saturday. Would you like to spend the night with Emily again? I'm sure they'd have you."

"Shouldn't we spend it with Mum?"

"I don't want you having to look after her."

What he means is that he doesn't want to have to look after her.

"She might not be your wife any more, Dad, but she's still my mum. Do you think I should ring her back?"

Lianne left Sarah's side as soon as she saw Ruth in the playground next morning. "Sarah says she really doesn't mind if you come and do the makeover party with us, Ruth. Go on! It would be great to have help."

Ruth glanced over at Sarah, who was trying – not very successfully – to look enthusiastic. Ruth was glad she had the perfect excuse, though she wasn't going to be too explicit. "Sorry, I'm afraid I've got to go to London to see my mum."

"She wouldn't miss you this once, would she?"

"Sorry, no can do. My dad's driving me up there tomorrow morning."

"Oh well," Sarah joined in quickly, "never mind. Another time. Do you miss your mum, Ruth? I would."

"So would I," said Lianne. "I'd hate to have to live with just my dad. Though I wouldn't mind having an older step-brother."

"Stop right there," said Ruth. "We're not talking about him. OK?" She'd spotted Matthew arriving in the play-ground and kept her head down.

Lianne had seen him too. She nudged Sarah sharply. Ruth saw how Sarah blushed, and realised in a blinding flash that Em had been right. Sarah, gorgeous Sarah, must actually fancy her pimply stepbrother! Lianne must know and that was the reason for the friendly moves as soon as Angela told them she lived there. A way to get in with Matthew. Well, well, well! What would he make of it?

"Gotta go!" said Ruth and ran off before they had a chance to say anything else.

Ruth

Matthew cornered me as soon as I got home. "OK, what did you say to them?"

"It's OK, Matthew, it's cool. We don't talk about you. Trust me. They're not interested." I was tempted to tell him that Sarah fancied him, and that he should be pleased, because Sarah is actually quite a nice person as well as being pretty, but I thought it better to leave well alone.

Lianne went round to Sarah's early on Saturday morning. The makeover party was later than usual – they weren't due until five o'clock, so they had plenty of time to get ready. "Which is lucky," said Sarah, "because I've had to hand-wash some of these clothes and they're taking for ever to dry."

"We're getting low on two of the hair colours as well," said Lianne. "Perhaps we'd better go into Boots this morning. We could have a burger for lunch."

Sarah sighed happily. This was just like the good old days.

Ruth

As we went up the front path, Dad said, " We'd better be prepared for Mum not to look so good, Ruthie."

Nothing could have prepared us. Mum took an age to answer the door. When she did, our house seemed dark and Mum looked like an old woman. All skin and bones and her hair sort of wispy and grey and uncared for. She had a strange, garlicky smell about her, too. Witchy. I shrank from hugging her, but I knew I had to.

"Look at me!" she said with a dry laugh. And I knew that's what she wanted Dad to do. To look at her and see what he had done to her. I could tell that he was shocked and didn't know what on earth to say.

"You two must have loads to catch up on," he managed in the end. "You go and sit down with your mother, Ruth. I'll make us all some tea."

"Hot water for me, please," said my mum to Dad, gazing at me. "Ruth, darling! My little girl! You seem so big and grown-up. I'm sure you've grown since you've been away."

"I doubt it, Mum," I mumbled. "It's only been about five weeks." Only five weeks and she'd shrunk almost to nothing. How could I have left her to wither away like that? How could I go away again?

Dad came in with the drinks and I could tell he wanted to talk to Mum on her own. "Gracie's in the kitchen," he said to me. "Fat old cat, just the same. I bet she's been missing you, too. I think you ought to go and say hello."

Gracie! My sweet, soft, fat Gracie-cat. Do you know? I literally haven't dared to think about her while I've been away. I'd have just missed her too much. I ran into the kitchen and swept her up into my arms. "Gracie, Gracie, Gracie!" I leaned my head against her purring flank and found myself crying. For Mum, for this dark house, for Emily who didn't seem to miss me any more, and for me.

Dad came into the kitchen. "Ruthie?" He stroked my head. "Phew. It is rather a shock, isn't it? I'm not sure what to do for the best. Do you want to stay over tonight? Or do you want to come back with me?"

"Oh, Dad! I wish you'd never –" I couldn't finish.

"What's done is done, darling." He sighed heavily. "But for now we've just got to try and do what's best. For you as well as your mum."

"Is she dying, Dad?"

"She will be if she doesn't start eating again," he muttered under his breath. To me he said, more gently, "In the end your system starts to pack up, but she hasn't reached that stage yet, not physically anyway. She's got the neighbours keeping an eye on her, apparently, so you go and be with her while I pop next door and find out a bit more."

"I want to stay over, Dad. Couldn't you sleep here too? Just for once?"

"Let me think about it."

"Mum!" I forced myself to hug her. "Mum, your hair is a disgrace. I'm going to brush it for you." I tried a bantering tone. "And have you been feeding all your food to Gracie? She's vast and you're positively anorexic!" Which is what she was, literally. "What does the doctor say?"

"Doctor?" said Mum. "The doctors aren't that interested in little old me. They refuse to believe there's anything wrong with me."

"Shall I make some soup or something for lunch? What have you got?"

I looked in the cupboards and there was hardly anything other than health shop pills. Mum shuffled into the kitchen. "There are a few packets of soup somewhere," she said, opening and closing some drawers. "From when you were here. I haven't thrown them away."

"Bread? Butter? Fruit?"

"I'll give you some money, sweetheart, and you can buy them from the corner shop."

"But what do YOU eat?" I asked her. "There's nothing here!"

"Oh, I get by," she said, sounding like an old crone.

I couldn't stand it. "Give me some money, then," I said harshly. "Lots. You can't expect me to stay here and starve with you. I haven't got a death wish, even if you have." I saw her shrink from me and felt cruel. But honestly.

Dad did stay. For my sake, not Mum's. He made that clear. I thought of Emily out on her date. Would she have changed it if she'd known I was in town?

Mum crept up to bed after toying with a baked potato. Dad and I watched terrible Saturday night TV. He phoned Angela at some point. I could hear him laughing and thought of the contrast and how glad he must feel to be out of it.

My room was just as I'd left it. I mean *just* as I'd left it, with the bed unmade and various clothes I'd not packed strewn across the floor. Mum used to be such a stickler for tidiness.

She obviously hadn't moped about in my room missing me. I took Gracie up and put the radio on and spent time trying to make the room as nice as it was in my memory.

In the morning, Dad and I got up first and had quite a cheery breakfast together. I took some tea up to Mum, but she said she only wanted hot water and she'd have that when she came down. When she did come down, she said lots about how well Dad and I seemed to get on – we obviously didn't need her. Well, what can you say?

"I'm going to see Emily. I need to get out for a bit." Perhaps I'd better ring first.

"Em? S'me."

"Roo!"

"So how was it?"

"Oo, Roo! He was so sweeet. I think I'm in love. I wish you were nearer, then you could come round and I could tell you all about it!"

"I am here. I'm in London."

"What? Why?"

"Mum's pretty bad. We thought we ought to see her. But she's no fun. Shall I come round?"

"Well . . ." She actually hesitated! "It's just that I'm about to go shopping with Hannah. I mean, it would be great to see you, but she's picking me up with her dad . . ."

Oh. "Oh well, never mind. I suppose I'll see you at half term."

"The week after next?"

"The week after that," I said.

"We must have different half terms, then," she wailed. "Oh, Roo, that's awful. I was so looking forward to being with you."

But she'd rather be with Hannah. That's great. Just great.

Chapter Nine

"Look, there's Ruth!" Lianne had seen Ruth striding grimly into the playground on Monday morning.

"So?"

"She doesn't look a happy bunny. Serve her right for not coming to our makeover."

"She couldn't. Anyway, it would have been hopeless with three of us, Lianne, you know it would. There was hardly enough room for us two."

The party had gone really well again. The birthday girl was a little sister of one of Maisie Johnson's friends and because the family lived in a tiny cottage, only six children were at the party. What's more, they'd been really well behaved and appreciative. Another fifty pounds for Miracle Makeovers.

Ruth came over, her mouth a tight line.

"Hi, Ruth," said Sarah in a friendly voice. "You went home this weekend, didn't you?"

"Yes," said Ruth, looking away. "Yes, it was cool."

"Geography this morning," said Lianne. "We get to find out more about the field trip."

"When is the trip exactly?" asked Ruth.

"The week after we get back off half term," said Lianne.

"We go on the Wednesday and come back on the Saturday – which is why we couldn't do the makeover that day. We don't get back until late."

"And there's always a disco on the Friday night," added Sarah.

They were piling into the classroom for registration. Anxious that some choosing of partners might be about to take place, Josie tried to squeeze in next to Ruth, but Lianne calmly told her to move her big butt out of it and Ruth, to Josie's chagrin, didn't even try to stop her.

"Everything all right, Sarah?" Mr Booth asked casually before registration on Thursday afternoon."

"Yes, sir," said Sarah in a colourless tone.

"Got something to look forward to at half term?"

"Going to my auntie's, sir."

"What's Lianne up to?"

"I don't know, sir, but I think she's going away somewhere with her mum and dad, too."

"And Ruth?"

"Don't ask me, sir. I don't know what Ruth does when she's at home. I don't go to her house."

The rest of the class pushed in past them at that point, but Mr Booth felt he was getting a shrewd idea of what was going on. It was almost as if Lianne was determined to have Ruth to herself, even at the expense of her friendship with Sarah.

Ruth

I don't know what's happening to me. Am I beginning to turn into a different person? I haven't checked my email or called

98

Emily – my supposed best friend – since getting back from London. Frankly, I'm not that interested in what Emily's up to with Hannah and Charlie. Especially now they're on half term. I haven't rung Mum. She's rung me but I can't be bothered to ring back. I just don't want to think about that life. I don't want to think about this one much, either. I just have to get on with it.

Lianne and Ruth were round at Sarah's house the last Thursday night before half term. Sarah's grandmother wasn't happy about the way Lianne seemed to be getting hold of Ruth. She was surprised, too. She had imagined that Sarah and Ruth could have been good friends. Ruth seemed a pleasant girl, less complicated than that spiky Lianne with all her schemes and money-making projects. Lianne and Sarah were avidly discussing their wardrobes for the field trip – Granny noticed that Ruth's eye's were glazing over (so she was still her own girl) – when Lianne's mobile rang. Lianne answered it, sounded puzzled and handed it over to Ruth. "It's some woman – for you."

It was Emily's mother.

Ruth

Emily's mother rang me up on Lianne's mobile. Spooky link from old life to new life.

"Emily's so anxious, Ruth, that I'm afraid I took it upon myself to ring you. Angela gave me this number – something about your friends doing party entertainment for Maisie?"

I remembered the smoothed-out flyer still pinned to the kitchen notice board.

"Can I ring you back? This is my friend's mobile, you see."

"Of course. It's just that Emily hasn't heard from you all this half-term week and she's getting herself so upset."

"I'll ring you back in an hour, from home, promise. Bye, Sue."

Lianne was looking at me questioningly. "Your number's on your Miracle Makeovers flyer," I told her. "It's been up since you came to the Johnsons' house for Maisie's party. I live there. You forget."

I decided to email Emily rather than phone. When I logged on, there were TEN messages from her. Angela said that she'd phoned twice that afternoon, as well, which was why, in desperation when Em's mum had finally rung, she'd suggested trying Lianne's mobile number on the Miracle Makeovers flyer. Emily's emails were all apologising for when I was in London, saying that Hannah and her dad had been due literally any minute, sorry, sorry, sorry.

And so on.

From ruth@yes.com
Em – I know that the flavours of the month are now Charlie and Hannah. Don't worry about it. I've got new friends here anyway. Lianne's a real laugh and Sarah is OK too.

Roo.

From Emily356@yes.net
Roo! Please don't go off on one. You have to believe me. I'm really glad you've got friends in Cobford, but old friends are IRREPLACEABLE, OK?

I've had this idea how we can see each other even though it's my half term this week and yours next week. It just so happens that Dad has a meeting not very far from Cobford tomorrow at four-thirty. We've looked at the map and he says he can drop me right outside your school gate on the way. So how's about I come down and visit you tomorrow and meet you and your friends from school? I'm dying to see it. Then I could stay over with you and do something Friday-nightish at your place and we could travel to London together on the Saturday. Mum says she'll meet us and everything. Go on, Roo, say yes – you know you want to.

From ruth@yes.com
    Em – Maybe. I'll have to see. Let me sleep on it.
    Roo.

Emily rang first thing on Friday morning. Dad answered, and of course he told her he thought it would be silly not to come and visit, since they were coming in this direction anyway.

"Roo, expect me outside your school this afternoon!" She sounded really excited, and so like old times I hadn't the heart to say no.

"Oh, OK then. We finish at twenty to four. This is where you get your dad to drop you . . ."

Lianne and Sarah were intrigued by the idea of Ruth's friend from London.

"Bet she's not as nice as us," said Lianne. "What sort of clothes does she wear?"

"Oh, ordinary clothes," said Ruth, imagining Emily in the slightly grungy stuff they both liked.

"Come to think of it," said Sarah, "we don't know what sort of clothes you wear when you're not in uniform."

"Nothing special," said Ruth.

"You will introduce us, won't you?" asked Lianne.

"Yes, you will, won't you?" said Sarah, quite pleased by the idea of Ruth having other friends.

That last day before half-term, the field trip was naturally the main topic of conversation or, more precisely, the clothes that everyone was going to take. They'd been told to bring warm and waterproof clothing with just one outfit to dress up in. Ruth was fine with that – she'd already decided to wear some of her mum's Eighties clothes for the disco. But judging from the discussions between Lianne and Sarah, every single item of clothing was of crucial importance. They were still going on about it as they bundled through the school gate that afternoon. Ruth was only half listening as she looked out for Emily.

Lianne spotted her first. "Ruth? That girl over there in the really long tatty jeans and sort of anorak thing? That's not your friend, is it?"

"Em!" Ruth shrieked and ran to hug her.

"Wo!" said Sarah to Lianne. "What *is* she wearing?"

"Another one who could do with a makeover," said Lianne. "Perhaps she has other qualities."

"She'd have to," said Sarah.

Ruth brought Emily to meet them. She saw Lianne and Emily look each other over. With loathing.

"Hi," said Emily. "I can't get over you guys all in uniform! Look at you, Roo! It's hilarious!"

"Thanks a bunch!" said Ruth, smiling, but she could see that Lianne and Sarah weren't amused.

"Most people think girls in school uniform look sexy," said Lianne, coldly.

"It means you don't spoil your other clothes," added Sarah.

"Well, I think it's a hoot!" said Emily. "Especially the ties! You look like traffic wardens."

"It's not *that* funny," hissed Ruth to Emily. "Anyway, see

you guys after half term," she said to Lianne and Sarah, and hugged them both before wheeling Emily round in the opposite direction for the walk home.

In fact, Lianne and Sarah were awaiting the arrival of Lianne's dad in a brand new car. They would cruise around Cobford in style.

Halfway home, Ruth and Emily caught up with Matthew. Ruth glanced around before greeting him and introducing Emily.

"So you're the famous Matthew!" said Emily, throwing her arms around him and kissing him on either cheek. "Almost family!" she said, grimacing over Matthew's shoulder at Ruth.

Ruth was transfixed with horror. Matthew might explode. He wasn't used to being hugged by strange girls.

But Matthew was surprisingly pleased. He ran his hand through his hair briefly, straightened his tie and said, "Which makes you the famous best friend. Hi. Call me Matt."

None of them noticed the shiny four-by-four with the newest registration gliding past. Tinted glass concealed Lianne and Sarah as they spied on Ruth a second time. But this time it was Ruth's friend Emily who attracted their attention, since she appeared to be in a clinch with Sarah's beloved Matt.

Lianne's dad drove on, unaware of the scene they'd just witnessed.

"Did you see that?" Lianne's mouth hung open. Operation Sarah-and-Matt was restored to centre stage now half term had begun and Ruth was off to London.

"Sadly, yes," said Sarah. "What's going on, Lianne?"

"I don't know," said Lianne. "We know *Ruth's* not his girlfriend, but that doesn't rule out Emily. Boy, are we going to give Ruth the first degree when we've got her in darkest Wales."

"That's not for ages yet," said Sarah.

"Don't worry, I'm sure there are other ways we can find out if Matt's got a girlfriend. Not that *Emily* would be any competition for you – once he knew you liked him." Lianne wrinkled her nose in distaste. "I bet those old clothes smell," she added.

Ruth

Emily seems to find everything hugely amusing. I got out of my uniform as quickly as I could, but she had to make comments about every single item. She couldn't resist tying the tie round her head. She thinks Matthew's completely hilarious.

"God," she said. "I see what *you* mean about Matthew being from another planet! His face looks like the surface of the moon for a start. And how long does he spend on that crazy hairstyle every morning?"

I suddenly felt oddly protective towards Matthew. The current moon craters were a lot better than the volcanic eruptions of a few weeks ago. "Oh, he's all right," I muttered.

"No he's not!" said Emily. "You're losing your good taste, my girl!"

What made it worse was that Matthew was obviously a bit smitten with Emily, a phenomenon I'd never observed before. He kept passing her things at supper. When she asked me how we were going to spend our Friday night in the provinces, Matthew started to offer suggestions.

"Well, thanks a lot, Matthew," I said sarcastically. "And where have you been all the other godforsaken Friday nights I've spent here, eh?"

"Out," said Matthew, with no sense of irony.

"Precisely," I replied.

In fact, the best he could come up with was going round to his friend Saul's house. I could see Emily wasn't keen, so I told Matthew we were really looking forward to a girly evening in front of the TV. There was a dodgy moment when he wavered, as if wondering whether or not to stay at home too. Emily was making frantic faces at me. "You go without us," I encouraged him.

"Oh, all right," he said, slightly relieved, I reckon.

Luckily Maisie was at gym club and Angela had to pick her up. Dad wasn't home from work, either, so Emily and I had the house to ourselves. Emily wandered round picking things up, looking at photos and generally casting a critical eye. "Don't know how you stand it, Roo," she said.

"Well, I don't have much choice, do I?" I'd forgotten how much I'd resented everything at first. "Anyway, it's not that bad."

"As for those girls . . . " she continued.

"Em, if you're going to go on about Lianne and Sarah – just don't. OK?"

Emily wasn't deterred. "Well, Sarah seemed all right, I suppose. But Lianne! Every strand of hair just so! Stupid tie just so! And she walks" – here Emily mimicked Lianne – "as if the whole world is watching her and admiring her. As if!" Emily had Lianne off to a tee. Usually, her impressions made me fall about laughing, but not this time.

"They're OK!" I said fiercely, suddenly feeling tearful. "And I don't have any choice about my friends, either. It's all right for you . . . "

Emily looked at me then. "Sorry, Roo. You won't believe this, but I think I was actually a bit jealous back there."

"You've got a funny way of showing it."

"Well, you know me. New friends and your very own step-brother. I can't compete." She hugged me.

"Shut up," I said, hugging her back. "Where's the remote?"

I'm sure Em was genuine, but I still felt hurt. It was all very well for her to waltz in on my new life and criticise everything, but not very kind. And Emily's always been kind up till now. We had got to a place we'd never been before, where I doubted her and she alternated between trying to be funny about every-thing and then apologising.

On Saturday morning when we were leaving, Matthew gave her an awkward hug and a peck on the cheek. I knew what that cost him, so I ignored the look of revulsion she directed at me. Dad and Angela drove us to the station, and I could just feel her storing up comments for later on the train, which she duly delivered. E.g., she thought Angela wore too much make-up for a weekend and made a joke about Dad's bald patch – all things which would have made me giggle along with her only a couple of months ago.

For the first time ever, Matthew saw that there might be some advantages in having a stepsister. Ruth's friend Emily was so open and friendly. She didn't giggle and whisper, like other girls. And she'd kissed him, twice. On the cheek, admittedly, but for a brief moment her lips had rested there.

Matthew rushed upstairs as soon as the girls had left, locked himself in the bathroom and inspected his face criti-cally in the mirror. His skin was massively improved, no doubt about it. It wasn't as smooth as a baby's bottom, but it was no longer the pustular disaster area that had earned him his nickname. He experimented with various winsome grins in the mirror. His teeth were OK. His dark hair had always been his best feature. And maybe he had quite nice eyes. Perhaps Emily had liked his eyes.

Matthew hugged this happy idea to himself. How great that Emily was nothing to do with school. And Ruth, when she came back from half term, wouldn't mind talking, just normally, about Emily. She needn't suspect anything, need she? Emily was her best friend, after all.

Ruth

Sue, Em's mum, met us and we went back to their house, which is such a contrast to Angela's. I've always taken Em's house for granted, but now I noticed how it was not smart, but lovely, much more homely than either of my homes. It's the sort of house that's full of books and magazines and music of one sort or another, where cats doze in comfortable armchairs. Emily has two younger brothers, both boffins. Her dad teaches at the university, so he seems to be around quite a lot of the time.

"Now, we really are going out tonight!" she said, as I unpacked my pyjamas and a clean T-shirt. "Dervla's older brother is having a party and you and me and Charlie and Luke are all invited."

"Luke?" I said. I hadn't known any other boys were involved. Not that I minded. I could get to like Luke.

"Yes," she said. "Luke's going out with Dervla."

So I'd be gooseberry then. "Do I have to dress up?"

"Nah. No one else is."

Well, Emily might not have been dressing up, but she was definitely getting very clean. She disappeared into the bathroom with two fresh towels and a whole load of tea-lights. The scent of roses wafted under the door as I sat on my bed and wondered what the evening held in store. When Emily eventually reappeared she spent a further age searching for matching underwear and then trying on six different tops. "You can borrow one of these if you like," she said.

"I thought you said we weren't dressing up?"

"You want to look nice, don't you?"

"What, nicer than I look normally? You're as bad as my Cobford friends, Em. So you think I need a makeover, do you?"

"Oh, lighten up, Roo! Try some of these on. We're meant to be having fun!"

She was right. I was being a bit boring. Normally I'm as happy as the next person to spend hours dressing up, but right now it reminded me too much of Sarah and Lianne and their obsession with clothes. I wasn't looking forward to going home to Mum tomorrow, either. Or to spending the week with her, while Emily and everyone else was at school. Or to going back to Dad's again. Or to the field trip. "OK. Give them here. How do I look in aubergine?"

I looked hideous in aubergine. I had a hideous evening. Emily disappeared with Charlie as soon as we got there. Luke couldn't even speak to me because he spent the entire time snogging Dervla. Dervla's older brother was seventeen and not one of his friends was the slightest bit interested in me, especially not me in aubergine. I wandered around the house until I found an unoccupied room with a TV and dug in for the long haul. I was woken at midnight by a frantic Emily who was meant to be back home by then – and would have been if she hadn't spent the past half-hour hunting for me. We got a cab and her dad was waiting up for us. Emily was full of apologies, but she laid the blame squarely on me.

"Don't worry," I said. "I'll be gone tomorrow."

Emily was yawning so hard, it was all she could do to say goodnight.

On Sunday morning I got up a full four hours before Emily did. Sue sat me down. "What would you like for breakfast? The works?"

She carried on asking me questions while she cooked. "How was it last night?"

"OK."

"Not too brilliant, then?"

I rustled the Cornflakes packet rather than answer that one.

"Emily misses you like anything, Ruth. I think that's partly why she's spending so much time with Charlie."

"I miss everything," I said and then felt too choked up to say any more.

"You know you're always welcome here, love. I've said so before and the offer's still there if you want be here in London without stopping your mum from having some space."

"Thank you," I said meekly.

Secretly I thought Emily would be bored having me there all the time. And I'd certainly be bored if she was with Charlie.

Sarah's dad was packing the last few things in the car for their half-term visit to his sister's when Lianne turned up.

"Won't hold you up," she said cheerily. "Here, Sarah, I've written a letter to Matt. Read it. What do you think?"

Dear Matt

Have you got a girlfriend? Please could you tell your stepsister so she can let us know.

From two admirers.

PS. If you don't, we might have some interesting information for you.

Sarah's jaw dropped. It was such a bad idea, and such a terrible letter, she didn't know where to begin.

"Are you mad? We can't possibly send this. Ruth would have a fit, for a start."

Lianne was stung. "You think of something better then."

"It's too direct. You know Ruth refuses to say anything about him to us." Then Sarah had a brainwave. "But Maisie might talk."

"OK. We'll nobble Maisie at the party next week. She's bound to be there."

"Good plan," said Sarah. "Anyway, I've got to go. Everyone else is in the car. Just tear up the letter. Bye!"

Ruth

Even though Mum was expecting me for half term on Sunday evening, she hadn't managed to buy any food. She didn't even seem that pleased to see me.

"I expect you'll try to bully me into eating more, just like everyone else, won't you?" she said.

Gracie was pleased to see me, but there was only one tin of cat food left in the cupboard. I realised I was going to have to be the grown-up here.

"Mum, give me your cash point card and PIN. I'm going up to the bank and then I'm going to the shop down the road. This is hopeless."

"Now you're going to get all cross with me," she whined.

"No, I'm not. I'm just going to buy some food. Come on – cash point card." I held out my hand. "It's a good job this is London and shops are open on Sunday evening. It's just a pity that the bank's so far away."

So often, just when you think things can't get any worse,

they do. It was six o'clock, dusk, and raining a wintry rain while I waited for the bus up to the Broadway – just the sort of conditions I wouldn't even have been allowed out in on my own a few weeks ago. First my hands started to get cold, then the rain started to soak through my jeans. The driver of the first bus chose not to see me and I had to wait another twenty minutes for the next one. I took out a hundred pounds on Mum's card and then waited another ten minutes for a bus home. I went straight round to the corner shop and loaded up with tins of cat food and all the stuff we needed to keep us going, like milk and bread and pasta and cheese and cereal. It was a ridiculously heavy load of shopping, but I slogged back to the house with it, cursing my mother, my father, Emily and the rest of the world on the way.

Gracie purred loudly as I dumped the dripping plastic carriers on the kitchen table and peeled off my wet jacket. I fed her and went up to my room to change into dry clothes. All this time Mum sat in a pathetic slump in front of the television. I cooked us fried eggs on toast for supper. She ate about a quarter of hers, so I finished it for her, and followed it up with two yoghurts. The house felt cold, so I went to turn the heating up. Mum had it on the lowest setting. She bleated at me that she couldn't afford to have it any higher – more jerseys was a cheaper way of keeping warm, but I ignored her. I quite wanted to watch Sunday night TV – Mum and I always used to watch what she called a 'good murder', but I really didn't want to share a room with her any longer than necessary – I was so angry.

Next morning I woke up with a bit of a headache. During the day it turned into a worse headache, combined with an awful sore throat and, by the evening, I had a temperature. I told Mum and she said 'not to infect' her because her immune system wasn't too good and that she wouldn't be any good at running up and down stairs after me. I rang Dad, who said I'd better stay where I was if I was infectious ... Honestly! I rang Emily for a moan and she was good to talk to for once – especially as it gave her a break from her maths homework – but even she said that she didn't really want to visit me if I had something catching. So I took a hot water bottle and the kettle upstairs, a carton of milk, some cereal, sachets of Cup-a-Soup, crisps, some squash and aspirins – and holed up in my room. Some half term!

I spent all Tuesday aching and shivering, yet burning up at the same time. Mum did fill up my jug of water then, and I knew she was worried, but she really didn't want to get close. By Wednesday evening I felt a bit more human and rang Dad again. He said he'd fetch me on Friday rather than waiting until the weekend. On Thursday I got up in the afternoon. I was hoping to catch up with Emily before I went back with Dad but, when I rang, her mum said she'd gone to Hannah's after school and was staying over. I could have rung Hannah's house, but somehow I didn't have the heart.

Dad arrived early on Friday. I was up and ready to go, but Mum hadn't appeared.

"She's often not up until about eleven," I told Dad. "But I want to say goodbye properly. I'll go up and see."

I knocked on her door before going in. There was no reply, so I put my head round the door. It was dark and airless. Mum's body was just a little hump in the bedclothes.

"Mum?"

She didn't move.

I felt a niggle of panic. "Mum?"

Still no reply. Suddenly I feared the worst.

"Dad!"

He raced up the stairs as I went over and shook her. She

wasn't dead, of course, but she looked tiny and curled up and felt hot to the touch.

"I must have got your flu," she croaked.

"Damn," said Dad – helpfully. "So what do we do now?"

"You flaming well stay and help me look after her," I said to him grimly. "What else can we do? She can't look after herself."

"Oh yes I can," she whispered throatily.

"You can't even look after yourself when you haven't got flu!" I sniped. "So I'll just have to unpack again, won't I?"

"But, darling," said Dad, "I have to work this afternoon. I've got a meeting. I really have to get back."

"OK," I said. "Go. Come and fetch me again on Sunday."

"Ruthie …" he cajoled. "Ruthie, darling. You do understand, don't you?"

"Not really," I said, hard as nails. "But don't bother hanging around, Dad. Don't worry about the fact that I'm still recovering from flu. I can manage without you."

So Dad went and I fetched Mum water and aspirins and hot water bottles. I even made her some real lentil soup, but she wouldn't eat it.

I rang Emily again on Friday evening. Her mum answered and said that Emily had gone to Brighton with Hannah for the Hallowe'en weekend, to stay with Hannah's older sister who was a student there.

I crept back to my room and howled.

By Sunday Mum's temperature was normal and I felt a little kinder towards her. In fact, I didn't really want to leave her alone again, but Dad was anxious to get us back and I had school in the morning, so we didn't linger.

Chapter Ten

Ruth

I hardly said a word to Dad as we drove back. I let him assume I was asleep, but really I was still seething at the way he'd left me to cope with Mum on my own. I was so worried about her.

Angela, Maisie and even Matthew seemed quite glad to see me. "Only for two days, though," said Angela. "Then you're off again."

"It's cool, that field trip," said Matthew. "We had a brilliant time when our year went." I realised he was trailing after me. "You and Emily get to London all right, then?"

"I wouldn't be here if we hadn't, would I?" If only he knew how rude Emily had been about him. Poor boy. He really is smitten. "Anyway, goodnight," I said. "I've got to get sorted for school tomorrow and think about packing for the field trip." I nearly told him that precious Emily had a boyfriend, too, but I knew Matthew didn't need to hear that, so I let it be.

Back at school all the talk was about the Friday disco. Even Josie was getting excited about dressing up. "It's got glittery bits all over the top," she was heard to say.

"With little lights round the bottom that don't work," Lianne added, making Sarah and Ruth snigger. "It's that swimming pool all over again."

"I've got a new waterproof jacket, too," said Josie, "with special pockets for everything."

"Perfect for the disco, then," whispered Lianne. "OK, Ruth, so what are you going to wear on Friday night?"

"I haven't quite made my mind up yet," said Ruth. "Whatever it is, I don't expect you to like it."

"As long as it's not manky old jeans like your friend was wearing," said Lianne, laughing uproariously.

"It could just be," said Ruth under her breath.

The midweek makeover party was straight after school the day before the field trip and Lianne had a mission to accomplish.

You really can't trust an eight-year-old to get it right. Sarah, being used to little kids, would have asked the appropriate questions, but Lianne went at it like a ramraider.

"That girl Ruth," she said to Maisie, "she's your stepsister, isn't she?"

"Uh-huh," said Maisie, jigging around, longing for it to be her turn to be made over again.

"Ruth's friend Emily is really pretty, isn't she?" Lianne carried on probing. "Your brother likes her, doesn't he?"

Maisie, who'd intuitively appreciated that her big brother fancied Emily, said dramatically, "They kissed!"

"So, is Emily Matthew's girlfriend, Maisie?"

Maisie quite liked the idea of Matthew having a girlfriend.

"Yes," she said innocently, eyeing up the sequinned top that she would wear when her turn came and hoping her friend in the chair didn't choose it first.

"I'm afraid they are going out," intoned Lianne gravely, as soon as she and Sarah could talk. "I asked Maisie. She said that Emily and Matthew kissed!"

Sarah was so crestfallen that she didn't think to query Lianne's methods of inquisition. "A scruffy London girl-friend," she said mournfully. "She is quite pretty, I suppose."

"Nowhere near as stunning as you, Sarah," said Lianne. "It's weird, though, isn't it, that Ruth never mentioned it?"

"Why should she?" said Sarah. "She doesn't know I fancy Matt, remember? And don't you *dare* tell her, OK? Thank God you never sent that letter is all I can say."

Later, when the two girls were waiting for Sarah's dad to pick them up, Lianne said dreamily and not altogether tactfully, "Perhaps Ruth's friend and Matthew have been marked out for each other since birth, you know, like an arranged marriage or something."

"You should have asked Maisie for more details," said Sarah.

"Well, we can ask Ruth herself everything in Wales, can't we?" said Lianne. "She's cagey about Matthew, but she won't mind talking about Emily. She's her best friend."

"I'm not gonna hold my breath," muttered Sarah as her father's car appeared round the corner.

Ruth

I'm packed. And for the disco I'm wearing, well, it's an amazing old outfit of Mum's from the bag of clothes she gave me before I moved to Cobford. I'd have paid a lot for that from a charity shop. Not that I can imagine Mum in it, of course. All black. The top has a wide neck and three-quarter sleeves, and the bottom looks like a skirt, but in fact it's culottes! Culottes! Trousers that look like a skirt! Nobody wears culottes any more, but I think they're fab.

I wanted to email Emily before I left, tell her that I wasn't impressed by her going off to Brighton for my last weekend in London, but my computer kept crashing. Dad is trying to make things up to me, so he said I could use his. I went into his study and turned his flash computer on. I spun around in his swivel chair while it was starting up and kicked over a tottering pile of books by mistake. One of the books was a photo album. I opened it.

How weird is this? It fell open at a photo of Mum wearing the outfit I was taking with me. She looked really young. With spiky hair! I don't remember her ever being like that – a healthy-looking human being, despite the white face and the dramatic eye make-up. Not the bag of bones she is now. She was at a party, happy, laughing for the photographer. I started to turn the pages. All the photos were of Mum and Dad. I'm sure it was from before they were married, maybe even when they were teenagers. I've seen wedding photos and they both looked older then.

Oh, Mum! How awful to turn from that into what you are now.

Dad is recognisable, but Mum seemed to be someone completely different. Was it having me that changed her? Was it my fault?

From ruth@yes.com
Scumbag! I can't believe you went to Brighton with Hannah without telling me. And me at death's door as well. Now I'm off to Wales and you might never see me again, because I'll probably fall down a pothole or something. I'm expecting an

email from you pronto to explain yourself.

R

PS. It had better be good.

Dad stood in the doorway. "Ruth, I don't want you to go off to Wales without hearing what I have to say."

"Fire away."

"I know you're cross with me because you think I should have helped you to look after your mum, but it's not that simple, darling. She's been playing games with me since long before the divorce. I don't expect you to understand and I'm sorry you had to get caught up in it, but I'm not prepared to join in."

"She wasn't playing at having flu, Dad. I thought she was dead! Remember? Someone had to look after her. So it had to be me, even though I felt pretty crummy myself. We're not talking about playing games here."

"Your mother is no longer my responsibility, Ruthie. We're divorced. I'm sorry, darling, but there it is."

"And I suppose I'm not your responsibility either? Fine! Why don't I just go and live on the streets, then?"

"Ruth, you know you're twisting my words. And I don't want to fight. I want you to go off on your field trip with your new friends and have fun. And not worry about your mother."

"That's not so easy, Dad. Especially if no one else is worrying about her."

Dad looked defeated. "So what am I supposed to do, darling? Bring her here? Angela would love that."

"Of course not! But you could make sure the neighbours look in on her once or twice? Or Sue? She did offer."

"Then Sue has to worry. But I suppose it wouldn't hurt, if it made you happier."

We had to be at school really early on Wednesday morning. So early that I didn't have time to check my email, and I still hadn't heard back from Emily. Maybe she'd have sent a rubbish excuse anyway. Dad said he'd drive me with my heavy backpack, and the others actually waved me off as if we were a real family. Matthew standing in the doorway carrying Maisie in her dressing gown. I felt jittery, as if I was leaving behind the only security I had. As if I was being cut loose.

"She *is* wearing tatty jeans and an anorak!" said Lianne to Sarah as they watched Ruth loading her stuff into the bowels of the coach.

"Just like Emily. It's obviously what Matt likes," said Sarah. "Perhaps I'd better start dressing like that!"

"I don't think so!" said Lianne. "As I've said all along, prime case for a makeover. Maybe this will be our chance."

The coach journey took nearly all day. Sarah and Lianne sat together. So did Ellie and Claire. Josie plonked herself down beside Ruth. It was going to be the same for bunk beds, walking partners, everything. Ruth sat back in her seat feeling desolate.

Everyone was relieved when they arrived at Caer Ysgol, the converted village school that was to be their home for the next three days. Ruth was in a dormitory with Lianne, Sarah, Ellie, Claire and Josie. Josie was thrilled because it was basically the 'popular' girls' room and would be the hub of all female activity at Caer while they were there. There was just time to unpack and wash before eating.

"Ask her about Matt now," said Lianne, shoving Sarah in Ruth's way as they were putting their clothes away. "No time like the present."

"Don't be daft," hissed Sarah. "Everyone would hear. I don't want Claire and Ellie earwigging."

Ruth sensed that something was going on, but she was too tired to care. Josie had begged to have the top bunk, a prospect that filled Ruth with gloom. Sarah hung around more than usual as if she wanted to tell her something, but Ruth couldn't think what it might be. She wasn't psychic.

"Maybe I'll be a bit more on the ball when I've had some food," Ruth said to her, yawning. "I can't see myself lasting much longer, though."

They traipsed down to a supper of sausages and chips and fruit salad and then on into the common room for talks from the organisers and Mr Bennett about their programme. Thursday would be rock formations and mountains, Friday would be coastal erosion, with a bit of caving and rockpooling thrown in. Thursday evening would be some project work and Friday evening was the famous disco. Ruth felt mildly enthusiastic about all of it, but the disco was the only event that was of any interest to most of the class. "Perhaps it's because I'm a city girl," she said to Sarah. "You lot are more used to countryside."

"Not mountains and sea, though," said Sarah.

"The beach will be cool," said Lianne. "Hope I remembered to pack my sunglasses."

On Thursday morning Ruth was cleaning her teeth and Lianne was putting on make-up.

As you do, thought Ruth, when you're going on a three-mile hike up a mountain. "You going to let me make you up for the disco then?" Lianne asked.

"Maybe," said Ruth.

"You OK, Ruth?" asked Lianne. "We're still mates, aren't

we? You've seemed a bit distant since half term."

"Have I? Sorry," said Ruth. "Got a lot on my mind." She wasn't used to concern from Lianne. It made her uneasy.

"By the way," said Lianne, glancing round, "Sarah wants to ask you something."

"Oh yeah?"

"Yes. Only she's a bit shy about it. Just so you know."

"OK."

They stopped to eat their sandwiches in full view of the rocky outcrops. The uphill climb wasn't something they were used to and a lot of people were complaining about dirt on their trainers. "I'm going to tell Sir how much mine cost," said Lianne, scrambling towards Mr Bennett and leaving Ruth and Sarah together.

"Ru-uth?" said Sarah.

Ruth prepared herself to listen. "What's up?"

"Well, the thing is – we wanted to know . . ." Sarah took a deep breath. "Well, something about Emily."

"Yes?"

"Yes. It's just that Lianne asked Maisie something the other day ?"

"Maisie? My stepsister?"

"Yes, she was at one of our makeover parties. We asked her if your friend Emily was going out with Matt."

"*What?* No way!" Ruth laughed. "No, no, no! Emily thinks Matthew's a complete pillock!" Ruth saw Sarah's face fall, and remembered that she was the one who fancied Matthew.

"That's not very nice of her," said Sarah.

"Oh, I don't mind," said Ruth. "I think he's OK. But we're not going to talk about him, not even here in Wales. He'd kill me. Change the subject!"

Lianne came back grumbling. "Sir just said we were told to bring sensible shoes for walking in and it's not his fault if we didn't do as we were told. A hundred and twenty quid! That's what these cost!" Sarah and Ruth looked down at their old trainers and didn't say anything. "I expect you're feeling smug," Lianne suddenly flung at Ruth. "There's nothing to spoil with your clothes, is there?"

Miaow, thought Ruth, but didn't reply. She packed her lunch away and walked on ahead.

Ruth

I can't believe they'd stoop so low as to ask Maisie about Matthew's lovelife! She's bound to say something to Matthew. Bound to. Just what he didn't want. And he'll think it's all my fault. What on earth made them think Matthew and Emily had a thing going? What has Maisie been saying? Little brat.

I thought I might enjoy this trip, but I'm not so far. It would be different with my old friends. A laugh, even. But not this lot. I just know they're watching me and sneering. I felt like an elephant in my lovely big jimjams. They're Dad's and I love them. I used to wear them when he'd just left home. I should have thought about it and got Angela to buy me some new ones for the trip. I wish Emily was here. I wish she was. The old Emily anyway. Sometimes Lianne can be funny, but right now I'm fed up with her. She looks so stupid pratting about in fancy new trainers and expensive jeans and a pale jacket. At least Sarah looks normal. Lianne's like a Barbie doll that has to have the right outfit for every occasion. Sometimes it seems to be all she cares about. I'm tired and don't feel well. This is how I felt when I'd just had the flu.

*

"You've gone and upset her, now!" said Sarah.

"Oh, not for long," said Lianne. "Anyway, I bet she does feel smug. I expect you do, too, come to that. Important thing is, did you get to talk to her? About what Maisie said?"

"Yes."

"Well?"

Sarah should have been pleased by Ruth's answer, but somehow she wasn't. With her own eyes she'd seen her beloved Matt being kissed by Emily. It pained her to think that he might care for someone who thought he was 'a pillock'. Poor, poor Matt. How *could* Emily think that? Sarah could see that Matt was moody and shy and that was part of what made him so attractive, along with his dark hair and his gorgeous eyes. Sarah sighed. Maybe it was time she kept her feelings to herself.

"Well?" said Lianne again.

"He hasn't got a girlfriend," said Sarah quietly. "I don't know why he was kissing Emily, but Ruth said Emily – that there's nothing between them."

"Wo-oh, girl!" shouted Lianne. "Way to go!"

"Shh," said Sarah. "Ruth might hear us."

"Good," said Lianne. "I know she's got the hump today, but I'm pleased for you. OK?"

"OK," said Sarah.

Ruth

When we got back to Caer, I told the other teacher, Mrs Prior, that I wasn't feeling too good. She took my temperature, which was above normal, but nothing too drastic. I told her I'd had flu last week and then given it to my mum and had to nurse her. She tutted away while she looked for aspirin in the cupboard and then checked some notes. "Well, Ruth," she said kindly, "I think some old-fashioned TLC is called for, don't you? How about you sleep in the sick bay tonight and then if you're feeling strong in the morning you can join the others again. Would you like to phone your mum, perhaps? Or your dad? I know being poorly can make you feel a bit homesick."

She looked round at me for an answer, but I couldn't speak. Suddenly I was in floods of tears.

"Dearie me," she said. "Would you like to tell me what's the matter?"

"It's just that – I wouldn't want to worry my mum, because she's – sick. And my dad . . . perhaps I should call him. He wouldn't be able to do anything though. Nor would Angela because of Maisie." I was rambling.

"Never mind just now," she said. "The others are going in to supper. I want you to go and fetch your nightclothes and come back here. I'll warm up the bed with a hot-water bottle and sort out some food for you."

"Thank you, Miss," I said with a snivel.

"Got children your age of my own," said Mrs Prior. "My son Robbie's here on the trip. He gets terrible asthma – can't breathe sometimes, so it suits me to come along." She saw me dissolving again and gave my shoulder a squeeze. "Run along, then."

"Where's Ruth, Josie?" Lianne prodded Josie's shoulder.

"She said she wasn't feeling well," Josie replied and quickly replaced her headphones so she could disappear back into her own little world.

"I told you you'd upset her, Lianne," said Sarah.

"Ruth's not *that* pathetic," said Lianne. "It'll be because she had the flu over half term. OK, maybe I was a bit harsh.

But we can make it up to her. I promised her a special makeover before the disco."

"That was nice of you," said Sarah.

"We sorted her uniform, didn't we?" said Lianne. "But there's her hair and her make-up now. She could look *so* much better." She reached for her nail file and rasped away at a nail that she'd chipped on the rocks. "And then, once she's looking fab and everyone tells her how great she looks, she might stop wearing those minging clothes. Honestly, Sarah, I couldn't believe it when she turned up dressed just like that awful friend of hers."

"Same here," admitted Sarah. "Perhaps it's a London thing?"

"A completely-lacking-in-style thing, if you ask me."

"Perhaps we could help her with her clothes, too. After all, Maisie loved it, and they are sisters, sort of."

"Now there's an idea," said Lianne.

Ruth

I'm in the sick room on my own with a pile of magazines instead of project work and I'm warm and cosy. I wish I'd had someone like Mrs Prior to look after me when I was ill last week! I think I can manage without phoning anyone tonight, but maybe I'll ring tomorrow. There'll be queues for the phone anyway because we weren't allowed to bring mobiles. Maybe I'll just snuggle down, read a magazine and get some sleep. I don't want to miss out on the seaside tomorrow. Nor the chance to wear Mum's brilliant old clothes. I wish I had them here – just the smell of them would be comforting. Never mind.

"Ruth's in the sick room," announced Claire.

"For the night?"

"That's what Mrs Prior said."

"Hey," said Sarah. "Maybe we should take a look at her clothes and see if we can do anything with them."

"That's not like you, Sarah," said Lianne. "You're usually all for leaving well alone."

"Well, I feel sorry for her and I think it would be a really nice thing to do. Anyway, I'm good at dressmaking, aren't I?"

"What's all this?" asked Claire.

"We thought we could do a makeover on Ruth. Make her clothes a bit nicer. You know? A bit more fashionable."

"Why stop at the clothes?" said Claire.

"We've already offered to do her hair and make-up," said Lianne.

"Getting rid of the glasses is what I meant. If Ruth had contacts, put her hair up and wore something smart for a change, she might even look like a human being.

"Ruth unpacked all her clothes," said Sarah. "Everything's in her chest of drawers."

By now all the girls, even Josie, were gathered round Ruth's chest of drawers. "Do you think we ought to be doing this?" asked Josie.

"Course!" said Lianne. "We're doing her a favour. Just imagine how happy she'll be to have the right clothes for the occasion."

"And we're professionals," said Sarah.

"I don't think Ruth would like it," said Josie bravely.

"Shut up, Josie. Go on, someone," urged Lianne. "Open the drawers!"

Claire opened the top one. It contained underwear. "Nothing wrong with that," said Claire.

Ellie opened the next one. It contained neatly folded T-shirts and jerseys.

Sarah opened the larger bottom drawer. On the left were two pairs of jeans, folded. On the right was an old C&A carrier bag. "That shop doesn't exist any more, does it?" asked Sarah.

"Nah, went out with the ark," said Lianne. "What's the betting these are smelly old charity shop clothes? Tip them out, Sarah."

Sarah stuck her nose inside the bag. "It does smell a bit – of scent, though. It's quite nice actually." She tipped the contents of the C&A bag on to Ruth's bed.

"They're a bit gothic," said Lianne. "They're all black! Yuk! You can really do something with these, Sarah."

"I've got a little sewing kit with me. Maybe I can buy some trimmings at the seaside town tomorrow," said Sarah thoughtfully. "Some little beads, shells maybe?"

"I know black's meant to be sophisticated," said Claire, "but you only wear it to a disco if it's sparkly, don't you?"

"I think black looks revolting on most people," said Lianne. "It does nothing for their skin tone. It certainly wouldn't do anything for Ruth's. I'll have to see what I can do with her make-up."

"What is this skirt thing?" said Sarah. "Look" – she held it against her – "it's a really silly length, and it's got – it's got legs!"

"Have to do something about that, Sarah," said Lianne. "Ruth's got good legs, she should show them off more. You could make it quite a bit shorter."

"Leave it to me," said Sarah comfortably.

"You'll have to work really quickly," said Lianne, "while I'm doing her face and hair."

"That's OK, but I think I'm going to have to do the cutting in the morning and just add the bits in the evening. You lot will have to distract her, make sure she doesn't take the clothes out before we all start to get changed."

There was a knock on the door.

"Stuff them back in the drawer," hissed Lianne, as everyone tried to look innocent. Sarah quickly closed the drawer and threw herself into the bottom bunk bed as Mrs Prior put her head round the door. "Big day tomorrow, girls. Settle down now."

"How's Ruth, Mrs Prior?" asked Lianne sweetly.

"That's nice of you to ask. I think she'll probably be all right in the morning, after a good night's sleep. I'm hoping she'll be able to make it to the seaside with the rest of you."

Chapter Eleven

Ruth

I really didn't know where I was when I woke up this morning. I felt loads better. Mrs Prior bustled into the sick room.

"You've been dead to the world, Ruth," she said. "This is the third time I've tried to wake you. You're too late to go with the others on the coach but if you're up to it, you can come with me and Robbie in the car at lunch time He had a terrible night. He had to sleep sitting up. Probably the spores in this old building."

I sat up and stretched.

"Have a shower and there'll be some breakfast for you when you're dressed." Wow. I could get used to being treated like this.

I went up to the dormitory, got out some clean underwear and had a shower. I opened the next drawer down and found a clean top. What about jeans? Would yesterday's be all right? I'd put them on the radiator, so at least they were warm and dry. They were only going to get muddy again. I decided to chance them. Thick socks, jacket, and I was ready.

Mrs Prior was very chatty while I had breakfast. She asked quite a lot about my family and somehow I didn't mind telling her.

I told her how worried I was about Mum, being all thin – starving herself really – and then having flu and she said something helpful. She said that maybe it would be good for Mum to be forced into seeing a doctor, or even going into hospital, because then everyone would know what was wrong with her and could help her get better. I hadn't thought of that. I was just terrified of her being too ill to look after herself.

"All the girls are talking about tonight's disco," she said. "I hope they're not too disappointed. The boys aren't nearly as bothered. I know Robbie would rather watch TV!"

"It's the getting ready they like."

"And what are you wearing?" she asked.

"Some of my mother's Eighties things. Black and cool. The skirt is culottes. Did you ever have culottes?"

"In my time," she said. "But not first time round. I'm not that old! Women found them useful for riding bicycles in the old days."

"These were just a fashion thing. I think fashions were much better then. I much prefer old clothes. Would you like to see them?"

"I'll look forward to seeing them tonight, dear. We haven't got time now. I need to get Robbie moving."

I'd honestly hardly noticed Robbie Prior before. I knew who he was, but our paths hadn't crossed. He was fair and pale and not very tall. But really nice. He talked to me in the car and sympathised about being new and having to get on with popular girls like Sarah and Lianne. "Do you like them?" I asked.

He looked sheepish. "I think Sarah is very attractive," he said (Bless!), "but Lianne's scary. In fact they both are. I was even quite scared of you."

That made me think. How could I ever be real friends with people if they were scared of me? And Robbie was a sweetheart. He'd be a nice ally to have. Was I scary? No one thought so at my old school.

"There's the coach," said Mrs Prior from the driving seat, "so your lot can't be far away."

"Hi, Ruth!" The four girls surrounded Ruth and seemed really pleased to see her.

"You didn't miss much this morning," said Sarah.

"Except we were allowed to go shopping in that little town," said Lianne.

"Exactly," said Sarah, quelling her with a look. "You didn't miss much."

"Oh. No, you didn't, " agreed Lianne, hurriedly.

"We got really filthy, though," said Claire. She looked at the others meaningfully. "You were right to put on yesterday's jeans, Ruth."

"Not much to spoil, eh?" said Ruth, forgiving Lianne, but sensing again that there was something her room-mates weren't telling her.

"We're going to have our sandwiches on the beach," said Sarah. "You're allowed outside and everything, aren't you?"

"Oh yes," said Ruth. "I think I just needed a good night's sleep. Mrs Prior brought me here with Robbie."

"That little squirt?" said Lianne.

"He's nice!" said Ruth.

"Yeah, right," said Lianne.

It was a good afternoon. At one point, amidst much giggling and embarrassment, Mr Bennett made everyone take part in a treasure hunt, boys with girls in pairs. Ruth paired up with Robbie and they won by a mermaid's purse and a razor shell.

It was great to act like kids again. Suddenly Ruth found she was almost looking forward to the disco.

When Lianne leaned forward on the coach to ask if she fancied Robbie, Ruth had the strength to tell her where to go. Robbie, sitting next to Ruth, felt braver too, and knelt up on the seat to chat to Sarah.

It wasn't just Ruth's immediate circle – everyone in the group was being more friendly to one another.

"We're giving Ruth a makeover for the disco tonight, aren't we, Ruth?" Sarah informed Robbie.

"What sort of makeover?" asked Robbie. "Ruth doesn't need a makeover."

"Hair and make-up – and stuff," said Lianne condescendingly. "You haven't forgotten, have you, Ruth? Sarah and I have got it all worked out."

"My outfit's so cool I won't need any help," said Ruth.

There was a moment's silence. A shocked silence, which Ruth would have noticed if she'd been feeling less cheerful.

"Only joking!" she added. "You did quite a good job on me last time, Lianne."

"All I care about right now," said Robbie, bored with makeover talk, "is food. Supper's at six, isn't it? Ten minutes. We'd better be nearly home."

After supper Lianne and Sarah raced upstairs before the others had left the table. "You've got to distract her, Lianne," said Sarah. "She mustn't look in her drawer for at least half an hour. Do you want to see what I've done so far?"

Sarah pulled the C&A bag from her own drawer and reached in her backpack for the bag of brightly coloured bits and pieces she'd found in the haberdasher's in town.

"Cool!" said Lianne. "Hope she's grateful. Quick, someone's coming!"

"I'll lock myself in a loo," said Sarah, gathering everything up. "See ya!"

Ruth, Josie, Claire and Ellie all arrived at once. "Bagsy first in the shower!" said Claire.

"I'll go in the shower by the loo, then," said Ruth.

"No, you go in the other one, Ruth," said Lianne, frowning at Claire. "And then I'll do your make-up. Don't wash your hair, though. It'll make it too hard to do anything with it."

"I'd rather just have it clean and loose," said Ruth.

"No," said Lianne, mock-bossy. "You're to do as I say."

"Oh, all right, bossy-boots," said Ruth, laughing.

When Ruth emerged in her dressing-gown, her hair was wet. "Sorree!"she said. "I'm just going to have to dry it. Where's Sarah? She brought a hairdryer, didn't she? Give me ten minutes, Lianne."

"Borrow mine," said Claire quickly.

Meanwhile, Sarah was sewing away in the loo. In her own way Sarah had done a very good job. She'd cut off and hemmed the three-quarter sleeves to make them cap sleeves and she'd turned up the bottom of the top to show Ruth's belly. She'd turned the culottes into a short, full skirt – which had meant about an hour's worth of hemming in the morning. She'd managed to buy pink and blue shell buttons and feathers, which she'd sewn round the neckline and dotted around the skirt. It certainly brightened up the black outfit and Sarah was immensely proud of herself. Lianne popped into the loo once or twice while Ruth was in the shower and was full of praise.

Now Ruth, hair clean and shiny, sat and allowed Lianne to make her up.

"Glasses off," said Lianne. "Put them there," she added, with a nod of her head at Claire.

Ruth

I suppose I don't mind a bit of make-up if it keeps them happy. If Lianne's really good, she'll make me look like me, only more so, and not like some stupid bimbo.

This afternoon's been fun, almost too much fun. Why do I get the feeling it can't last? Mrs Prior and Robbie made me feel like myself, my real self, but with everyone else it's as if I'm playing someone else. I don't really want Lianne to be doing this, but I'm letting her. I just wish I could stop worrying, about Mum and home and Matthew and Emily and what's to become of me. Where do I belong?

Josie came in. "Phone call for Ruth," she said. "Downstairs."

"Who is it?" Ruth sounded panicky. "Where are my specs? Oh, never mind. I'll just be blind." She rushed downstairs, still in her dressing-gown.

"Easy!" said Mr Bennett as she ran into him at the bottom. "Phone's through there. Young man called Matthew for you."

Ruth

"Matthew? What's happened? What's wrong? Is something the matter with my mum? Do I have to go home?"

"That's not why I'm ringing you. Your mum's in hospital, but you're not supposed to know that."

"WHAT?"

"She's OK."

"But?"

"I'm ringing because I've got a very big bone to pick with you, Ruth Miller."

"What? What do you mean?"

"I want to know what you've been saying to your friends to make them cross-examine Maisie about me and – and – Emily, that's what I want to know."

"What?"

"Oh don't come over all innocent. You must have said something about me first. So now those girls think they can discuss my personal life with Maisie – even though she's just a little kid. What else do you talk about with your friends? What other juicy titbits have you been passing on, eh?"

"MATTHEW! You pompous git! Shut up! I can't help it if one of 'those girls' fancies you. Yeah! Sarah – not Emily! I can't help it if Lianne chooses to pump Maisie. I wasn't even there, for God's sake. And I couldn't care less, either. What the hell has happened to my mum? Get me Dad now or I'll go straight upstairs and tell Sarah exactly what sort of underpants you wear, even about the Superman ones ... And the zit cream."

I was shaking all over. I've never shouted at Matthew before, but how dare he have a go at me and just mention, as an aside, that Mum's in hospital?

Dad, Dad, come on!

"Darling, I can't believe Matthew phoned you in Wales. He never said a word to us. Mum is safely in hospital being looked after. Emily's mother persuaded her that she needed some help. They're keeping her in for a few days. We'll go and see her when you get back. She's in good hands. In fact, now you can stop worrying about her."

I couldn't think of anything else to say. I was furious and worried, and all my insecurities came flooding back. I stomped back up to the dormitory.

"Ruth! Ruth!" everyone was saying. "Put your disco clothes on!"

"Wait a sec," said Ruth. "I need my glasses. I haven't seen what Lianne's done to my face yet." She walked over to the mirror and peered into it.

"This isn't really – me, Lianne," she said, looking at what Lianne had done with the eyeliner. "And the lipstick's – kind of – a funny colour."

"But you look great," said Sarah encouragingly.

"Well, I don't feel great," said Ruth, lifting things off the chest of drawers in an effort to find her glasses. "My effing stepbrother! The cheek!"

"Oh," said Sarah. "What?"

"Nothing," said Ruth. "Where are my specs?" She was starting to hunt more frantically. "He just rang me up to have a go at me – because Maisie's been asking questions. Can't think why, Sarah. Lianne?" Ruth glared at them. "And he only happened to mention in passing that my mum's been taken into hospital . . ."

"Get ready for the disco and forget all about it, I should," said Lianne, ignoring the fact that Ruth was on the verge of tears.

"Huh," said Ruth, and turned to her bed.

Ruth couldn't believe what she saw lying there. She drew in her breath sharply. She stared at her mum's ruined clothes in stunned silence. Everyone else fell silent too. Ruth started quietly, dangerously, her voice rising with each howl of disbelief: "What have you done to her clothes? You've cut them up! You've sewn appalling pink and blue feathers on to Mum's culottes. YOU'VE CUT THEM UP!"

"Do – do you like them, though?" asked Sarah, helplessly, even though it was quite plain that Ruth didn't.

Chapter Twelve

"Oops," said Lianne.

"I don't think 'oops' quite covers it," said Ellie.

"Oh, come on, Ruth," said Lianne. "Sarah has worked really hard to make these look nice for you."

"Oh, it was Sarah, was it?" said Ruth, leadenly. "Gee, thanks, Sarah."

"Try them on!" Lianne was still determined. "You'll look great, honestly. Cooler than anyone else at the disco.

"I think it'll look brilliant," said Claire. "We all know how good Sarah and Lianne are at makeovers."

"Yeah, right," said Ruth, still stunned.

"Please, Ruth!" Lianne wouldn't let it go. "We've done your make-up and your hair and everything. Please try the clothes on."

Ruth didn't reply at first. "Where are my glasses?" she asked. There was a general murmuring.

"Where are my GLASSES?" Ruth asked again with gritted teeth. "I can't see without them. What have you DONE with them?"

"Er, they're here." Claire produced the glasses from her top drawer.

"You *hid* them?" Ruth was incredulous.

"Well, you see . . . We sort of thought if you saw how nice you looked without them, you might . . . you might . . . decide to get contact lenses instead," Claire tailed off lamely.

Ruth stood up and roared at them. "How can I SEE how good I look if I'm blind? Huh? Tell me that! And how sodding PATRONISING can you get? I don't happen to think I NEED a makeover. I don't WANT to look like you lot! I LIKE my specs – they were really expensive, since that seems to be all you care about! How DARE you cut up my clothes – my mum's clothes – and hide my glasses! How DARE you!"

Ruth was really screaming now. She pushed her glasses up on her nose and held her dressing-gown tightly round her. "You chose the WRONG PERSON for a makeover, OK? The WRONG PERSON!" And then she threw herself face down on the bed and bawled.

Ruth was beating her fists on the pillow and crying, "I want to go home! I want to go home!" when Mrs Prior came in. The other girls were still standing round in shocked silence. Lianne spoke first. She held up the altered clothes – quite proudly.

"Honestly, Miss, we were only trying to help. Sarah worked really hard on that outfit. It took her an hour to sew round the bottom of the skirt. They were trousers before, Miss."

Mrs Prior realised that she was looking at the beloved culottes. "You do realise, don't you," she said icily, "that you have cut up and ruined – *irrevocably* – an outfit that was precious to Ruth because it belonged to her mother?"

"Sarah has made it nicer," said Lianne. "You should have seen it before, Miss."

"Shut up, Lianne!" said Mrs Prior. "Sarah, you should be ashamed of yourself."

"I am, Miss," whimpered Sarah. But she couldn't help adding, "We thought they came from a charity shop."

"And we're not just amateurs, Miss," Lianne carried on. "We're professionals. We know what we're doing. Ruth was going to look fabulous."

"So you know what you're doing, do you, Lianne?" said Mrs Prior, her voice heavy with sarcasm. "I think not." She sat down on the bed by Ruth. "Ruth, I think I'm going to settle you in the sick room again. We'll leave these stupid, stupid girls to ponder what they've done for a little while."

She helped Ruth to her feet and walked her to the door, where she turned back to the others and said sternly, "I will deal with the girls responsible for this outrage in due course. That you can be sure of." Then she took Ruth downstairs.

Ruth

I didn't want to be this victim person all of a sudden. I could see the way the others were looking at me, but I'd run out of energy. And I trusted Mrs Prior. I felt she'd stand up for me and be on my side, even if I decided I wanted to forget all about what had just happened and go back to being best friends with Lianne and Sarah.

"They weren't to know," I said weakly when she'd sat me down again.

"They went too far, whether they understood what the clothes meant to you or not. And I really would like you to speak to one or other or your parents tonight. I think they should know what's going on."

This set me off again and I told her about my phone call from Matthew and that Mum was in hospital. And that was when I found I really couldn't stop crying. The thought of Mum made me cry and so did the thought of Dad and Matthew. I felt so sorry for myself that everything made me cry.

Mrs Prior made me get into bed, make-up and all, and fetched me another hot-water bottle. She obviously believed in hot-water bottles. I think I do, now, too.

"You really shouldn't have hidden her glasses, Claire," said Lianne into the silence.

"Look who's talking, Lianne! You thought it was a good idea yourself, you know you did."

"Well, I just wanted her to look nice, I didn't want to make her blind."

"Oh be quiet," said Claire.

"What's going to happen to us?" wailed Sarah. "I feel terrible."

"Don't be such a wimp, Sarah," said Lianne crossly. "They can't do anything to us. I still think she should have been grateful."

"OK guys," said Ellie. "Disco time!"

"Yeah, let's just forget about Ruth Miller, shall we?" said Lianne.

"You lot go," said Sarah. "I'll come along in a bit." When they'd all gone, Sarah went downstairs and phoned home. She felt very confused – about Ruth, about Matt Johnson, about Lianne, and she needed to hear the sound of her mum's voice.

Meanwhile, another phone conversation was going something like this:

"Mr Miller, is there any way you could drive down here tonight?"

"Would that really be any use, Mrs Prior? It would take me four or five hours, so I wouldn't be there until midnight."

"I suppose you're right. It's just that I think your daughter needs a parent right now. She's very worried about her mother, quite apart from the problems with the other girls."

"I thought she was making friends?"

"Not very thoughtful friends, I'm afraid. But I think it's anxiety about her mother that's at the bottom of all this."

"Matthew really shouldn't have told her."

"It would certainly have been better coming from you." Mrs Prior had the feeling she was dealing with one of her pupils. Mr Miller didn't seem to want to take responsibility for anything. She gave an exasperated sigh. "Obviously I'll look after her. She's no trouble. But I think it would help if she could visit her mother in hospital as soon as possible."

"I suppose it will be the weekend tomorrow. I'll see what we can do." At least she'd extracted that out of him.

Robbie sat on Ruth's bed. "Aren't you going to the disco, then?" he asked cheerily. You look very trendy in your dressing-gown, though I think I prefer you without all that make-up. What happened to the makeover?" Mrs Prior came back in and told him that it had gone wrong. It had been a very bad idea. "You should come to the disco, though, Ruth," he said. "I need someone to talk to."

"Nothing to wear now."

"You don't have to dress up! Wear your jeans."

"I'm feeling pretty wobbly. It might not be a good idea."

"Why don't you just go for half an hour with Robbie?" said Mrs Prior.

Ruth went upstairs. It was deserted with everyone at the disco. She changed into some clean jeans and wiped all the make-up off. She brushed her hair loose. Someone had put the ruined clothes back into the C&A bag, so at least she didn't have to look at them.

It was almost dark in the hall where they had the disco. Ruth and Robbie crept in the back. Lianne and some of the girls were dancing, but the boys were just chatting and looking on.

Sarah was in the loo. Crying made her make-up run. She splashed cold water over her face and tried to get a grip on herself. She'd got Granny on the phone instead of Mum and, of course, Granny hadn't had much sympathy. "That poor girl," she'd said. "Really, Sarah, what came over you? I suppose Lianne had a hand in this."

All Sarah wanted to do now was to let Ruth know how sorry she was, but Ruth wasn't there – she'd been taken away to the sick room. Sarah wondered if she'd ever see her again. What if Ruth hated them all so much she had to go back to London? And it was all Sarah's fault. Certainly Matt Johnson wouldn't ever be interested in someone who could be so cruel.

But Sarah wasn't a cruel person. She had genuinely thought she was doing something kind – that Ruth would really appreciate a makeover, just as Lianne had loved the one they gave her at the magazine. Just as she would have loved it.

She stood up straight, wiped her eyes and blew her nose one last time before going back to the hall.

And there was Ruth! Standing with funny little Robbie Prior, but looking just like herself, with her glasses and jeans and her hair loose. As if someone had put the clock back and the last horrible hour had never happened. Sarah took her courage in both hands.

"Ruth!" she croaked, cleared her throat and tried again. "Ruth?"

Ruth looked over at her guardedly.

"Ruth! I just want to say that I'm really, really sorry. I didn't want to upset you, honestly I didn't. I didn't realise . . . and Lianne . . . Anyway. They're punishing us."

"Are they now?" said Ruth. She didn't seem in a mood to forgive.

"They phoned our parents. No school trips of any sort for a while. It's the same as if they'd caught us smoking or drinking."

"Oh," said Ruth.

"I hope you don't think I'm an awful person," said Sarah.

"You mean," said Ruth, "that you hope I won't tell Matthew that I think you're an awful person? Don't worry, Sarah. He's just as bad. You'd probably suit each other."

"No! I mean –" Sarah looked wild-eyed. "How did you know? That I like Matt?"

"I'm not as stupid as you and Lianne think I am," said Ruth coldly. "Come on, Robbie, I think I've been here long enough."

Sarah watched them disappear into the light, and her eyes filled with tears all over again.

"Well done!" said Robbie. "That was telling her. I think Lianne's the real culprit, though."

"D'you know, Robbie? I don't really care any more. I just want to go away and leave all this behind. And if I can't?

Well, I'll just have to grin and bear it, I suppose. But I don't have to *care*."

They'd reached the corridor that the sick room was in. "Anyway, thanks for your company. I'm going to bed now. 'Night."

" 'Night," said Robbie, feeling worried.

There was a buzz of concern around Ruth the next morning when everyone got on the coach, but she sat in the front and stared ahead. She looked pale and hid behind her hair and her glasses as she had at the beginning of term.

Further back, Sarah sat with her head bent, cowed and frightened about doing anything bad ever again. She could sense already that she was going to be eased out by Claire in Lianne's world and she wasn't sure that she even minded. She wanted to be back home with her family, somewhere where she didn't feel such a totally evil person.

The coach pulled up outside the school as dusk was falling. There was a smoky, bonfire-night smell on the air. Parents and brothers and sisters were milling about.

Lianne's father was there, ready to be angry with her. Sarah's mum was there with the two little ones. As Sarah rushed to meet them she bumped into two people waiting for Ruth: Mr Miller and – Matt. "Sorry – sorry," she said, appalled, shaking her blonde head and looking up at Matthew with frightened eyes. Little did she know that that would be the moment he looked at her properly for the first time and felt almost overwhelmed by how pretty she was.

Ruth was surprised to see Matthew there with her dad. "Matthew wanted to apologise," said Dad. "Didn't you, Matthew?"

"Yeah, sorry," he said. "I was out of order. I sort of knew your mother was safe in hospital and I forgot that you'd be even more worried."

"Huh," said Ruth.

"OK, OK," said Matthew as they got into the car, casting a glance back at Sarah. "I know I shouldn't have rung you anyway. Things got to me. That's all."

"Huh," said Ruth again, but she managed an almost playful punch on his arm. "Everyone seems to want me to make them feel better about themselves," she said. "I really don't understand what I did to deserve any of this in the first place."

"Angela's got a nice supper in your honour, Ruth," said Dad. "And I'll take you to visit your mother tomorrow. That Mrs Prior certainly knows how to make a parent feel he's been neglecting his responsibilities!"

"Lots of practice, I expect," said Ruth, realising that her father also wanted her to make him feel better about himself. "And now I'm going to go and check my email."

Chapter Thirteen

Ruth

From Emily356@yes.net
Hi Roo!

Sorry I didn't get back to you before you left. I was going to phone, but then it was too late/too early sort of thing. It was my mum who got your mum into hospital in the end, and she says it's far, far better that she's being looked after. More about that later. Thing is, I just want to say (all embarrassed now) how much I miss you. Hannah's fine and Charlie's (er . . .) interesting, but I'm not ready for the big relationship thing yet. I WISH you were here. Do you really have to stay in Cobford? You can still come and live with us, you know, and then you could keep an eye on your mum. (My mum says she reckons your mum must miss you much more than she's letting on.)

So. What a lot of missing, huh? Hope Wales was fab. Reply when you get this.

Emxxxxxx

From ruth@yes.com

Ems

Wales was a total disaster. Dad's taking me to visit Mum in hospital tomorrow. Can we come round after lunch?

I made a little goody bag for Mum: recent photos of me and one or two old ones of her I begged off Dad including the one in the outfit; some soapy smelly things I had left from my birthday and a little book of love poems I had two copies of. And her favourite sort of chocolate almonds.

I don't think I've ever been in a hospital before. The smell was what hit me first and then all these ancient yellow people in wheelchairs and on the beds. We walked down this long, long corridor, Dad and I, dreading what we were going to see. Dad held my hand tightly. I was prepared for Mum to look terrible, but actually she looked much better than last time – they'd been making her eat in hospital. She was on a psychiatric ward in a cubicle on her own. It wasn't very nice and there were some strange people around, but she seemed calm and almost happy. Chiefly she was pleased to see me. Dad didn't hang around.

I was so relieved to see her looking more normal. I hugged and hugged her, and she hugged me back and we both snivelled a bit.

"What's going to happen next, Mum?"

"They're keeping me in for a while, darling. They don't trust me to eat properly on my own, yet."

"If they're making you better, Mum, that's fine by me."

"Sue's been fantastic. She says Emily has been lost without you this term. I suppose I have too."

"It hasn't been a barrel of laughs for me either." I decided not to talk about Lianne and Sarah and my so-called makeover. Apart from anything else, Mum might not have been too happy about having her old clothes cut up. When I'd asked what was going to happen next, I actually meant about ME, but I could see that Mum wasn't thinking beyond herself just yet. "Who's feeding Gracie while you're away?" I asked, to change the subject.

"Ros and Andy next door. They've been very kind." She thought for a while. "How was your geography trip?" she asked at last. "Where was it?"

"Wales, Mum." How weird that my own mother didn't even know where I'd been. "It was OK," I said, deciding to spare her. I suppose I've had to protect her a lot since Dad left.

It was Mum's lunch time and a nurse said it would be better if I went home now, because they didn't want her distracted and because Mum needed a rest after lunch. I kissed her goodbye and promised to visit again very soon, though I wasn't sure how I was going to manage that one.

Dad was waiting in the foyer for me. "Quick sandwich. Drop in on Emily and then whizz home, OK, love? There's stuff I've got to do this afternoon."

"Sarah, guess what?"

"Surprise me."

"I had all these messages on my mobile when I got in last night. We've got two more makeover parties. One's for an eleventh birthday party. What do you think? The clothes will be too small, but we can do good make-up. Perhaps we could take our own clothes along . . . "

"Uh-huh," said Sarah.

"You could sound a bit more enthusiastic. Two gigs come to a hundred pounds. Maybe we should buy some charity shop things and you could work your magic like you did on Ruth's clothes."

"I can't believe you just said that."

"Oh, come *on*, Sarah. We're building up a reputation! We're doing well. And just think! Every time Maisie Johnson comes home raving about another brilliant makeover party, Matt gets to hear your name!"

"I *really* can't believe you just said that."

"Lighten up, Sarah."

"Thing is, Lianne, I'm not so sure about all this makeover business any more. You know, the principle of it?"

"I don't want to hear this, Sarah. Now think about it very hard because, if you want out, I can think of at least two other people who'd like in. Know what I'm saying?"

"I know exactly what you're saying Lianne. I'll tell you tomorrow what I decide."

Ruth

"Roo!"

"Em! Thank you for my email. It made me feel a lot better. I've had such a hideous time, Em. I'll have to tell you all about it. You were right about Lianne and Sarah. You'll never guess what they did to me!"

I told her. It was so good to talk to Em. She made me see the funny side. "I know Sarah did the actual deed, Roo, but I bet it was Lianne who set her up."

"I forgot to tell you. In the middle of this I met a nice boy."

"You dark horse, you. What was he like?"

"I'm only teasing. He was a nice boy. About four foot nothing. Asthmatic. His mum was the teacher who looked after me and he was just – nice. About the only nice person I've met."

"Roo?"

"What?"

"Come back. I've been talking about it with Mum. You really can live here while your mum's in hospital and you can visit her. There's a bus, but my mum would drive you there. You can feed Gracie. We'd all love it."

"D'you think I could? Would it be like running away?"

"Who cares?"

"I used to be really angry with Mum, Em. But I'm not any more. She loved my dad more than he loved her, I think. Dad doesn't like being responsible for people – he's told me often enough. Angela's tough and she managed on her own for ages before she met him, so he doesn't have to feel responsible for her. But I want to look after Mum now. Well, I want us to look after each other."

"Then stay with us, till she's out of hospital. Then you can go back home. Go on. Let's talk to our parents about it."

"Dad, I really don't want to go back to Cobford. Nothing against Angela and you, not really. But I'd just so much rather be here. It was always Mum's idea, not mine, that I lived with you. Nobody asked me, remember?"

"I'll have to think about it, Ruth. It's rather a shock. Matthew and Maisie will be disappointed."

"Yeah, right."

"No need for that tone of voice, Ruth."

"I think your dad will be disappointed," said Em's mum gently.

I gave him a hug. "I love being with you, Daddy," I said. "But I prefer living in London. It's you versus Mum and all my friends and life here. You and those cows at school."

"OK, OK," he said. "I suppose I can't say no."

"D'you mean I can just stay? Now? And never go back to that school?" Happiness flooded through me. Em and I grabbed each other and jumped up and down.

"We'll have to make arrangements with the schools," said Dad to Sue.

"I'll help with that," said Sue. "Emily says that no one new has taken Ruth's place. I'm sure it won't be a problem. Anyway, if she's living here, they'll have to educate her somewhere!"

"I'm so happy, Dad! Can I go over and see Gracie now?"

"Lianne?"

"Hi, Sarah! Have you come to your senses at last? Guess what! Matt Johnson was hanging around the shop when I helped Mum close up last night. What do you think all that was about?"

"Actually, Lianne, yes – I have come to my senses. I don't want to do Miracle Makeovers any more. I'm really sorry to let you down, but –"

"What! And kiss goodbye to fifty quid?"

"It's not the money, Lianne. It's just the idea that you can change people by altering what they wear and . . . and stuff."

"You can. And little kids love it. And we make money out of it!"

"Yeah – but what we did to Ruth. I'll never forget her face. Kids should feel happy with the way they are."

"You're very holy all of a sudden!"

"If you say so."

"Well." Lianne huffed and puffed. "Well! Claire is dying to come in on it with me."

"I said I didn't want to let you down. And I won't if Claire can't do it, but you did say . . . "

"Ever more holy. Saint Sarah. Pardon me for living."

"Lianne!"

"See you next week."

"You Sarah?"

"Yeah." Sarah felt herself blushing furiously.

"I'm Matt. You did a party for my sister? My little sister." He swallowed. "You know my stepsister too. Ruth?"

Sarah held her breath. Was he going to have a go at her, like all the others?

"Er – do you fancy going to the cinema some time?"

Sarah's jaw dropped.

"Sorry. Never mind. I'd only wondered. Sort of."

"No, no!" said Sarah. "I mean, yes! Yes, I'd love to. Whenever."

"Yeah? Whenever. Cool," said Matthew. He hitched his bag over his shoulder and walked on.

Ruth

Gracie was cross with me at first, but when she'd eaten her food she came and sat on my lap in front of the TV and purred and purred. I'll go back to Emily's soon, but for now it's nice to sit in my own house and be myself. I'm still going to spend some weekends with Dad, so I'll see Matthew and the others sometimes. Dad's going to get me a mobile, so I can text them all. I never want to see Lianne again, but Sarah was OK really. Perhaps I'll give her a call some time ...